LADY LAWYER: SMALL TOWN JUSTICE

BY: SHELLEY L. LEVISAY

SHELLEY L. LEVISAY

*To all attorneys fighting to defend the
Constitution and civil liberties*

CHAPTER 1

They told you how hard it would be to make it through law school. They never told you it was just the beginning. Those of us in solo practices constantly hustle for clients. The old saying, "You eat what you kill," applies. It's not the glamorous life you see on tv. You don't graduate law school and walk out making your six-figure income with Armani suits and wealthy clients lining up. It's not like that at all. It's a hustle. It's a constant state of trying to get more clients and trying to get paid.

My name is Lindsey Jones. I am thirty-two years old and as a young woman, I must fight even harder. If it's not male attorneys calling you "Babe" or "Hon" or asking you to get coffee, it's clients that talk down to you like they know more than you. One of my favorite memes online is a coffee mug that reads, "Your google search isn't the same as my law degree." I'm primarily a criminal defense attorney. That area is still a male dominated field. Outsiders' feelings are that it is too dangerous for women to be around all those criminals. People often ask me, "Surely, you don't like going to those jails?" In the Bible Belt in particular, women are supposed to be prim and proper right? Even my own family disapproves and wishes I either did corporate law or worked in a firm.

The truth is, I like my criminal clients. They are normal people who either never had a chance, made a stupid decision, or didn't think at all. No one likes visiting a client in jail or prison: leaving your electronics in the car, being searched, and being locked in until the guards get around to letting you back out or bringing you your client. But with the downside of criminal law, comes the excitement. We get the memorable cases: the cases everyone wants to hear about, and the cases that make the news-rarely does a probate make the news!

Divorce cases outside of Hollywood rarely make the news either. What the public doesn't know is that lawyers are more in danger in divorce or custody cases than in any other type. You are messing with people's money and their children. People lose their minds during divorces. Anyone that practices in the dreaded family law will tell you that if they get another call that their ex is fifteen minutes late for visitation, they will pull their hair out. Another favorite is, "My ex cheated on me and I want something done!" What people don't realize about "no-fault divorce" is that no one really cares anymore. Judges will hate you if you start making them be the bedroom police. If I billed for every call, text message, email, and pleading you must file in family law cases, it can be quite lucrative, but I'm too nice to do that.

It may sound cliché, but I went to law school to help people. I wanted to be the champion of civil rights and of women and children and the poor. It's all great in theory, but in practice, that doesn't pay the bills. People think there is some safety net that pays lawyers. I wish there were, but there really isn't. I hear the same excuses day after day as to why someone can't pay. The same story that the drugs or gun wasn't mine or they can't prove it was me. A big part of what I do is manage expectations. Everyone thinks you get to take your case to trial and get to tell your story from the beginning, but you don't. In fact, if you are not a prosecutor, you don't get to tell your story unless you go to trial. I as a defense lawyer, haven't done my job if we go to trial. The reality is, most of my clients are guilty, but even so, their lives are in my hands.

These people don't know me outside of reading my website or an ad somewhere, yet they trust me with their lives, their freedom, their kids, their property-the things that matter most! It is easy to get jaded, but it's a great power and like the quote from Spider-Man, "With great power comes great responsibility." The worst part of my job is dealing with the clients. It would be easy without them and it is so easy to get jaded doing case after case, but occasionally, someone gets to you. Typically, it's when push comes to shove, and it is time for trial.

I can't explain it, but a trial is an experience unlike any other. When you are in a jury trial, your life revolves around that trial. You eat, sleep, and breath it. On average, I have 200 or 300 cases at any given time, and I better remember everyone's names and their facts in my head. You don't get weeks to prepare. You get experience and you learn to prepare quickly, or I hate to tell you, you won't make it as a trial attorney. I love trials! The adrenaline rush of speaking to that jury. The strategy of it. The drama. I love everything about it. Except the waiting for the verdict. That is absolutely the worst part!

My heart pounds and pounds, as those jurors file back into the courtroom. The adage you hear on tv that if they look at you, it's not guilty, and if they don't look at you it's guilty, is simply not true. There is no way to know. Sometimes you can think you know what they will do. You think they will vote this way and they just don't. You have twelve non-lawyers deciding your fate. To a lawyer it is frightening, but most of the time, juries get it right. Defense lawyers lose most of the time, but again most of the time the people are guilty. But what about the wrongfully accused? It's so hard to know if a client is truly innocent or not. Most of them claim they are innocent right until the end. It's easier with the ones that come in and say, "Yes I did it. Get me the best deal possible." Those that profess their innocent, you would think would be the greatest, but it is scary, and you just never know who is telling the truth.

There are times I absolutely don't believe them, but I cannot put on false testimony. Everyone thinks we don't have ethics, but most of us really do. Just like there are bad doctors or bad teachers, there are bad lawyers, but those are the exceptions and not the rule. If someone confesses to me, I cannot question him on the stand knowing he will lie. The experienced criminal knows this, and they will spin every story in the world as to why they are innocent. You may absolutely believe in your bones that they are lying, but it gives the client the choice to take the stand and tell that tale.

So, you may be thinking why do I do it then? Day in and day out. The long hours. The difficult clients. The suspense of it all. Why do I do it? Because I absolutely love it and wouldn't want to do anything else. Researching the law and forming arguments and attacks is fun-well at least to me. Getting to save someone from having a criminal record at 18 years old for being stupid is a good feeling. Helping a woman leave an abusive relationship. Helping someone get visitation with their kids. Helping a childless couple adopt a child. All those things revive and restore me.

Another thing that I love is the camaraderie with other attorneys. Every docket in every county where I practice, I meet fellow lawyers and there is an unspoken bond because we have shared some of the same experiences and have shared problems. A group of us commiserates together regularly, and those friends help me persevere. First, Nick, though 25 years older, is a true colleague and friend. Mariah, another mentor, has been a court appointed attorney for her entire career. Tyler, one of those lawyers who may have crossed that line a time or two, is one you can't help but love. Will, the one with no filter, who is shockingly highly intelligent, but has decided to run for district attorney this year. Last, but not least, Micah is the philosophical one.

Several more attorneys practice in our county, but it's like high school with the cliques and caricatures and stereotypes. But through it all and despite sometimes aggressive and almost violent fights in the courtroom or in politics, a bond ties us all together. And no, it isn't greed or money. It's a belief in the law-in the Constitution. A belief in Justice, that elusive concept that so many times we fall short of in our world, keeps up going and we keep trying. That's why we don't give up.

Despite this general spirit of congeniality, this year our bar is more fractured than normal because there is a hotly contested campaign for district attorney as the previous one has announced his retirement. Currently, his first assistant-who none of us can stand-has announced his candidacy against my friend Will that I mentioned earlier.

CHAPTER 2

My office is across the street from the courthouse within a building full of offices-really the best location for a lawyer. I have built in bookcases that sit behind me full of legal statute books and other legal scholarly books. I have two desks that form an L shape. The side desk holds my computer with two screens and a printer. The front desk faces clients.

It's Monday morning and the grind starts up again. Manic Mondays as I call them. You have: the rush of new client calls, the current clients calling because visitation didn't go well this weekend, and the girlfriend calling about her boyfriend's DUI arrest over the weekend. It all becomes normal to you after a while.

Prior to entering private practice, I was a prosecutor, and then the Defendants were never real people to me. They were names on a page. I didn't understand them. I certainly couldn't relate to them. Now having switched to the other side, if I ever went back, I would be a much better prosecutor now. Every defendant has a family. Every one of them has a story.

That's how I found myself meeting with this newest client. I'm meeting with his mom Glenda about her nineteen-year-old son. Just a kid. He's charged with one count of murder and one count of attempted murder. His parents aren't rich. He is facing life in prison. A public defender will encourage him to plead out. He did shoot the people. Police caught him trying to flee the scene with a bullet in his back.

"Lindsey, I've heard that you are a really good attorney-a former prosecutor-and that you care about your clients and work with people on payments. I can't lose my son. He's all I have. I'll pay you every month for the rest of my life, just please help me. His bond is $300,000 and I can't afford to get him out."

"Ma'am those are serious charges. When does he have court next?"

"They just came and arrested him one Saturday night with guns blazing and ten different police vehicles. He went to court that Monday and the judge said he was facing life on each count. Then, he went back last week with a court appointed attorney and he said the offer from the State was thirty-five years. He would be fifty-three. That attorney set it for a hearing that is next month. Matt tells me it wasn't his fault. This happened nine months ago, and nothing happened. Why did they just now do something?"

"I don't know I would have to look into it." I begin typing on my keyboard looking up the case of the State of Oklahoma v. Matthew Flowers. I see he is set for preliminary hearing the next month. "Has he ever been in any trouble before?"

"Never, but he has gotten into drugs. I don't know much about them, but he was staying up for days at a time and not keeping a normal schedule, but he's a good boy. He wouldn't ever have hurt anyone unless he felt threatened. He's never even been in a fight. My son is not violent. From what I heard, the people were bad people-like in with a gang or something. I just don't want my son's whole life to be ruined over this."

"Let me meet with your son and look into his case, but it sounds like he may have a methamphetamine addiction and just know being under the influence of that drug can often change someone's personality. How much would you be able to put down towards my taking this case?"

"I brought $1500 which is everything I have saved up, but I can pay you something every two weeks when I get paid. I promise I will. He's all I have. Please work with me."

Against my better judgment, "At least $200 a paycheck and any costs you have to come up with that as well."

She jumps up, "Thank you, thank you. Can I give you a hug?" Embarrassed, I stand up, "Sure, and I will do everything I can to help your son."

I send her out to pay my receptionist and I start the initial paperwork-an entry of appearance to indicate that I am representing the defendant (the jail will need that before I make an appointment to visit him) and a discovery motion requesting that the D.A.'s office provide their police reports and evidence they have against my client. I copy and take to the court clerk's office for filing. I love all the court clerks in my county. They are so kind and helpful. They usually ahead if the office is not too full—I can say that not all counties are like that! That is an advantage of a small-town bar and smaller local courthouse. I file my documents, check my courthouse box, and grab my correspondence from other attorneys and judges. Then, I stop in and see my favorite bailiff Sherrie. "Hey Sherrie, how are things going?"

She smiles. "Pretty well, except I can't get over this cold. My daughter has a basketball tournament starting tonight. Here's the latest Avon catalogue, I'll be placing another order next week."

"Great. Typical Monday where I'm trying to catch up from the madness over the weekend. Do you have the felony docket ready yet?"

"Just finishing. I'll print you a copy." I hear the printer start up.

"Thanks, I better get back at it. Later, girl."

I stop off at the D.A.'s office, which is on the top floor the courthouse, and give them the entry and discovery motion and wait on the police reports. Then, I walk back across the street to my office. Several of us in my building share a receptionist, Lea, but she is technically my employee. I hate answering and returning calls to anyone, not just clients. If I can get away with texting, I do. She usually handles all my scheduling and mailing.

I have another assistant Emily, that works for me part-time as needed. She always files, but sometimes I have her take paperwork to other counties to file or call and collect unpaid legal fees. The other solo practitioners and I all try to band together and help each other the best that we can with covering appearances or sharing documents. Emily is one of those pretty women: the kind who always has her nails done, always has perfect make-up, the pretty blonde hair like a mode, and of course a large chest. She is younger than me but has two kids. She's easily a mean girl as an adult, with men coming in and out of her life, but she does a respectable job for me and I trust her.

"Lea, will you call the jail and try to schedule an appointment with Matthew Flowers for tomorrow at 3?" I hand her the file.

"Sure, but I will probably wait until after lunch since it's so close."

"That's fine. I'm going to lunch and then have court in another county so I'm not sure I will make it back today," I go into my office and get my files for the criminal docket in a sister county. Nothing exciting but this is a typical day for me.

CHAPTER 3

My day starts with a temporary order hearing regarding custody. I represent the father, who hasn't seen his child in two months. The judge presiding over this case is the Honorable Judge Steven Clarkson, who presides over majority of the domestic or family law docket. The Governor appointed him after the last judge retired, having been on the bench for a decade. This is an elected position typically, but the prior judge left mid-term, so a committee chose his replacement. He came from the D.A.'s office prior to taking the bench, like way too many of our judges. Assistant District Attorneys are often in court more than any other attorneys and form bonds with the sitting judges and other lawyers because they admire their public service. The problem with prosecutor judges is that many times they have never practiced any other type of law and have no experience handling divorces or personal injury cases or breach of contract cases and get on-the-job-training.

The courthouse is decades old with marble floors and a large picture of the President hanging next to a flag when you approach the stairs. The courtrooms I practice in are not the cushy ones you see on tv. The tables, chairs, and pews squeak and are uncomfortable. The air conditioners are like the ones you would find in motels. It is often frigid or feverish in the courtrooms. They are outdated and lawyers must bring their own technology to court. Some judges don't even like lawyers to use their tablets in court to take notes.

Mom's attorney calls his client who accuses my client of several instances of domestic violence, but police have never arrested my client, nor did she bring any proof of any marks or bruises he caused. While Mom also makes claims that she has concerns about Dad's marijuana use, ironically, the District Attorney recently charged her for possession of methamphetamine. But anytime allegations of domestic violence raised, visits are typically supervised for some period, but his mother is supervising, so not a bad result. The Court orders my client to an evaluation, and if it turns out a professional counselor does not think he has an issue, I will probably be able to get him unsupervised visitation moving forward.

Now, I head back to the office to pick up new divorce cases that I worked on last night to take to the courthouse to file. Most of my paperwork I prepare at night or in the evenings because most of the day I'm either in court or driving to and from court appearances. I practice regularly in six counties and several times I will attend court in three counties a day. I text my process server that I have two more serves. I then get Mr. Flower's file back from Leah and read through the police reports before I meet my new client.

They buzz me in when I get to the county jail, and I head to the administration office to sign in and show my license and bar card. I take my legal pad and file only with me as I go back to meet my client. A guard ushers me back to a room that locks behind me until they bring me my client. A few minutes later, my client comes into the room cuffed and in orange coveralls. The guard cuffs one hand to the chair and leaves one loose so he can sign paperwork. He looks so young: tall, blond, and baby-faced. He's medium weight, so he hasn't been strung out on drugs too long—none of the normal signs of gauntness, sores, missing teeth, etc. He's still a good-looking kid. I extend my hand. "Hi Matt. I'm Lindsey. Yesterday, your mom hired me to represent you."

"Hi, nice to meet you. Thank you so much! I don't think that public defender was going to help me. He said he could get me twenty-five years on Murder Two, if I waived this next hearing. I told him, 'No, it was self-defense,' but he wouldn't listen to me."

Next, I give him my usual spiel, "Matt, everything you tell me is confidential and privileged. I cannot reveal it to anyone else without your permission. It is helpful for me to know the truth and the facts so I can appropriately defend you and not be blindsided, but I can't lie-despite what people say about lawyers. I can't present something in court that I know not to be true. Also, I caution you to talk to me and only me about this case. Not your cellmate. Not your girlfriend. Not your mom. No one over the phone. The prosecutor can use any of that against you, and I have seen jail phone calls torpedo cases. I've read the police reports, but you tell me what happened from the beginning."

"Look, I went over there with a buddy of mine that night."

I cut in, "Who was the buddy?"

"My friend James. He knew Aaron and Rachel."

"Why were you going there? Just tell me the truth. I've read the report and know that Aaron has been charged with trafficking in drugs and possession of a firearm after former conviction of a felony."

"We were going to get some shit."

"By shit, I assume you mean methamphetamine?"

"Yes."

"How much did you do?"

"First, we were going to buy a quarter ounce, but then we came in and started hanging out. Aaron loaded a bowl and we all did some. Then, James got a call and left me there saying that he would come back and get me. We were just chilling for a while and Rachel loaded a needle and asked if I'd ever shot it. I hadn't, so I tried it. It threw me for a loop, and all of us were high. Aaron started saying that he heard people outside and thought someone was trying to break in. He kept looking through the blinds and checking the surveillance. I looked out too and didn't see people but saw flashing lights, so I thought there were people out in the country around the house. I did think I saw movement on the surveillance monitors. Aaron goes into another room and get his 9mm and hands his girlfriend her .22 pistol. He tells her to stay inside and he and I would go check around outside. We go outside and at the time I could swear that there were people out there hiding. When I sobered up, I don't think there was anyone there, but I thought they were after this Aaron guy. So, I said, 'Hey dude I'm just going to go ahead and go.' Then Aaron pointed the gun at me and yelled, 'You're not going anywhere. Those are your people out there. I'm not a punk. You're setting me up. You're not gonna rob me and get away with it.'"

I put my hand up. "Hold on let me get caught up here. Why did James leave? Did you know these people?"

"No, this was the first time I met them."

This is part of that world I just don't understand. Hanging out in someone's house that you don't know and doing drugs with them. It is a part of that addiction and disease. "Did you bring a gun?"

"Yeah, I have my conceal carry permit. I always carry my Glock with me."

"Where was Rachel when Aaron pointed the gun at you?"

"She was in between us at that point. I was near the door because I was going to leave. Aaron was on the other side of the room. Rachel was sitting on the couch to the side."

"What happened after he pointed the gun at you?"

"I told him, 'Chill out. I don't even know you. I just came to get high. I don't know where James went or why he left.' But while I'm saying this, I grabbed my gun from my waistband so I would have it if I need it.

Then Aaron said 'Rachel, go lock up the stuff in the safe.' She grabbed all of the baggies of drugs and took them back to another room and then heard a loud bang that sounded like a gun shot at the time, so he rushed to my side of the room and looked out and I pulled my gun out. By this time Rachel ran back in as well and said, 'What was that?' Aaron answered, 'They are coming for us. This guy is their inside man.

He pointed the gun at my head, but I fired at him first and hit him in the upper chest/shoulder region and knocked him down. Rachel screamed and fired in my direction but missed. I fired back and hit her in the stomach. I run out the door then.

Next, I heard more gun shots ringing out. I crouched to the ground and zig zag, but I felt a stabbing pain in my back. I kept going for a couple steps before falling to the ground. It seemed like I laid there forever before I heard sirens and I eventually pass out."

"That's quite a story. The report says that there are video and audio recordings of interviews of you and of the alleged victims, including one by her in the hospital before she died. They don't have to provide those yet, but we will get his testimony on the record at the next hearing and go from there. Do you think he will show up and testify against you?"

"I hope not. I've got some people trying to find that out."

"Be careful with that. I would prefer you do nothing, or you could be facing an intimidating a witness charge on top of everything else." I stand and tell the guard through the speaker that we are finished.

"Nice to meet you Matt. Here's my card. My cell phone number is on the back. I have an account set up on that phone number to accept jail calls. If something comes up, call me, but remember these calls cost, so don't just call to chat."

"Thank you, ma'am, for helping me." He shakes my hand again. With that, I leave the interview room and wait for a guard to escort me back outside the jail. I'm a little claustrophobic and hate not being in control, which you never are in a jail. I can't imagine staying here for any appreciable amount of time.

CHAPTER 4

I am managing this district attorney's campaign for Will for a couple reasons. First, our community needs a change. Second, I personally know from my time at the district attorney's office that they no longer need to be in charge. District attorneys have so much power. They can ruin people's lives by signing a piece of paper and it sometimes goes to their heads. My mind flashes back to the past,

THREE YEARS EARLIER

"Lindsey, Michael wants to see you in his office," the receptionist says through my intercom. *The boss is actually in today. I wonder what this is about.*

I headed downstairs to his office, and he motioned for me to have a seat and shut the door. "Lindsey, you know I like you, but simply put none of the other prosecutors like you. You're pissing them off. You need to dumb it down."

What? Why would anyone want me to dumb it down? This is who I am. I'm the geek-the smart one. What I actually ask is, "I'm sorry what exactly is the problem? Is there a specific case or something that I have not handled correctly?"

"No, not exactly, but the guys feel like you should be coming to them for advice and asking their approval on your cases. You're doing well and the judges all say as much, but your colleagues think you're a know-it-all and you need to recognize that you are still a new attorney. So, appease them and start asking questions even if you think you know the answer. In general, they just don't like you personally, but I'm tired of hearing the complaints."

"I didn't know being popular was a job requirement."

"Make amends with them and try to become one of them

and maybe ask why they don't like you and calm the sarcasm and maybe don't talk as much. Hope it works out because you work hard but my prosecutors need to all get along and your supervisor not liking you may not bode well for your continued employment."

This is ridiculous. I work hard make way less than any of the rest of them and carry on a caseload of 1000 cases and file more charges than anyone. All the judges say I'm the best trial attorney in that office except for Michael. So, what if I don't socialize with the other ADAs? I have nothing in common with them. They want to talk about sports or their kids. I don't really like sports and don't have kids. In all honesty, I like kids in small doses and don't plan on having any myself. Of course, he doesn't get it, he isn't here enough to know what goes on in his own office.

TODAY

Tyler, Will, and I meet for lunch to discuss the campaign. We have a former legislator who now works as an advocate for criminal justice reform that is on board and helping us. Our other major helper is prominent citizen and on the board of most of the non-profits in town. I formed an agenda to keep us on board: specifically, what events we need to attend and how much money we need to raise. We've been attending every event imaginable as well as door knocking every weekend and any weekdays that we can. Fundraising and managing social media can be full-time gigs. We have a few attorneys supporting us, but all the power player attorneys are for the first assistant and have been less than generous in their assertions about our abilities, but we believe in the cause.

This campaign fills all my free time outside of work, much to the chagrin of my husband Justin. Justin and I met in high school and I realize now why everyone says not to marry your high school sweetheart. We are different people. We've grown apart and are roommates now. He's as intelligent as I am and ambitious, but he's also immature. It took him six years to complete his bachelor's degree, but he couldn't really find a job with a history degree, so he switched and got a master's in business. Now he's an accountant. He makes decent money, but our lives seem to have gone in different directions.

This isn't how I pictured married life. I thought we would have all couple friends and do everything together. Not so, and as I learned more about myself, I need a certain amount of time to myself. He's into sports and wants to spend all his time going to football and basketball games and still wants to do the college scene of socializing. I'm over that if I was ever much into it to begin with! I love my work. My life seems to revolve around it. I love him, but lately I'm more energized working or hanging out with other attorneys. It's not that I want to be married to someone else. I'm just more independent than I thought I would be. I make far more than he does. I feel like I do more of the housework and plan most, if not all, of our social calendar.

To be fair, he does help with things, particularly takes care of the cars and the yard and occasionally cooks, but we just don't connect anymore. He doesn't like my friends and won't come hang out with them. I don't really care for his, so we end up doing different things. We do watch tv and movies together. Our one thing we continue to do together. We don't go out. We usually order in food or one of us cooks dinner. My phone goes off at all hours and this leads to another one of our arguments because I take the call.

"Do you really have to take calls at dinnertime/ You work all the time. You care more about your clients than you do your husband."

"Justin, I have a large felony docket tomorrow. I need to talk to these clients. It'd be nice if they communicated more regularly but they don't. These people's lives are in my hands. I can't just ignore it."

"Whatever. It's always something with you." He goes back into the living room and turns on the television.

My clients need me. It's not like he's working to keep the romance alive. Sure, he wants to have sex, but when was the last time he planned some romantic night out or did something sweet to show he cared? Too long for me to remember.

I clear my plate and take my briefcase in the living room as well and pull out my iPad and start working in there with him while we watch tv. I try to start up a couple conversations, but he ignores me, so I just stay quiet. All our pets are in here with us-two dogs, named Cinder and Dallas, and two cats, named Ricky and Lucy. I pet the cat that is situated behind my head on the couch. We don't have children. To be honest, I'm not sure I want children. I love them, but in small doses really. Children change your life, and I'm not sure I could continue my career the way it is if I have children; so, the dogs and cats are our children. One of the dogs is a German Shepherd and one is a Rottweiler. One of the cats is a white Persian and the other is a long-haired black cat.

I look around my living room and shake my head thinking that this is my life. Life is not like television or a movie. Not even close. I remember back when Justin and I were sixteen and both of us were so shy and awkward: took a few months before we even had our first kiss. Back then he was so sweet and attentive: he wrote me notes every day sometimes more than one a day. We held hands everywhere we went. We wanted to spend every moment we could together: we didn't have to do anything, but just be together. You can't duplicate that puppy love experience. I still love him, but back then any time away from each other was utter torture. We were so innocent then: eating ice cream together, going for walks, and dreaming of the future. We didn't know what adult life was like but couldn't wait to get there. We both had all these plans to take over the world.

CHAPTER 5

Today, I have a felony pre-trial docket. I head inside the large courtroom and it is full of anywhere from 150-200 defendants and 10-30 attorneys for all the defendants. The defendants in custody surround the attorneys along with all the files in their orange jumpsuits. This docket is like a cattle-call with attorneys and their clients lining up to make their "ready for trial" announcements. All of our usual suspects of the defense bar is present, and we are shuffling paperwork and calling out our client's names to see if they are present and getting them prepared, while also trying to catch the ADA who has our case and make some last-minute deals. Many times, we don't get to talk to the ADA before the dockets or they aren't worried about it until they must address it because of their heavy caseload. Ninety-five or ninety-seven percent of cases are resolved with the defendants entering a guilty plea in exchange for a deal we negotiated with the D.A.'s office and if that weren't the case the dockets would be backed up for years and the justice system would come crashing down and to a screeching halt.

Nick is there with his several clients. "Hey Lindsey, how are your negotiations going?"

"Well I'm setting several for trial or blind plea (meaning the judge decides the sentence and it is not an agreement between the D.A.'s office and the defendant) at this point and some non-payers I'm filing motions to withdraw. How about you?"

"I'm trying to continue things out as far as we can until after the election and maybe get some different results. Have one lady back there brought $20 with her after three months of not paying. She gets to wait until the end of the docket so I can get out of her case. The nerve of these people: they are facing prison, but let's not pay the lawyer whose job it is to keep them out of prison."

"Yes, I have one that brought $40, but promises will have more on Friday. That doesn't help me today. Part of our street law, you know. The election may definitely change things when we get some more programs in there.'

Another reason that I'm campaigning for Will is that he is running on criminal justice reform-a political ideal that is thankfully taking hold across the nation. The incarceration rates in this country are outrageous and the overpopulation in the prison only contributes to giving non-violent criminals a master's education in crime. Our current first assistant who runs everything many times has overruled the other assistants when we have deals worked out and setting some arbitrary rules about no probation for certain crimes or refusing programs to defendants he just doesn't like.

The next jury term is about three weeks away, and at this point, I still have seven trials set. Only two or three of mine may go during that term. Unlike many attorneys I love taking cases to trial. Defense attorneys, unfortunately, aren't likely to win, but if you can save years in prison for your clients, you have achieved a victory. If the state offered your client twenty years in prison and at a trial, the jury only recommends ten years, then you have saved your client a decade behind bars. Your client can return to his family a decade earlier and that is huge. Most citizens and prosecutors do not think about the defendant's families when they send someone to prison. For example, the likelihood that his or her children may go into foster care, and a defendant may miss their whole child's upbringing. Sometimes, their parents or grandparents die before they are released, last seeing them in prison or in a courtroom. Rarely does a defendant get to attend a funeral. If a defendant is lucky enough to have a spouse stick by them, the fact that that person only gets to see their loved one weekly, and that is if they can afford to travel to the prison wears on the individual and their family. I forgot to mention the cost of phone calls or food for their loved ones in prison, which is an exorbitant money-making scheme.

The one I think I will try this term is for one of my drug dealers. Most drug dealers are not these kingpins that you see on tv driving the fancy cars with the fancy suits. Many of them are addicts themselves that started dealing to support or feed their own habit, and if you are using quite a bit of your own product, you are not making all that much money. This one I look forward to taking to trial because I have a defense. The police found the drugs on his female companion and not on him.

Micah is also on this docket and comes over. "Looks like I may be taking this one to trial after all because the D.A.'s office is insisting on prison for a client who was caught with large amounts of baking soda."

I look at him with a raised eyebrow. "Come again? When did possession of baking soda become a crime?"

"They filed it as felony endeavoring to traffic cocaine arguing that the client thought it was cocaine so he should still go to prison. There's a misdemeanor case that would fit and I told them my client would plead to probation on a misdemeanor and they aren't interested. I don't see a jury sending him to prison for possession of baking soda." He's shaking his head

"Yeah, that's ridiculous. Good luck with that one. I might come watch part of that trial. I'm going to be trying a drug trafficking case as well. Nick represents the co-defendant who was caught with the drugs but is going to testify against my guy, but it's a rather good case for me."

"Sounds interesting. Any other cases you think will go to trial for you?"

"Have some others set, but probably that and a termination of parental rights case."

I signal to five of my clients to get in line so I can schedule their plea dates and another three to announce ready for trial. I look over and see Mariah shaking her head. "Not getting anywhere with them either I take it?"

"No. Apparently eight people can cultivate a marijuana

plant and neglect children whenever the marijuana was in a locked room in the garage and need to go to prison over it."

"I wonder how that's going to work when our clients have medical marijuana cards and can grow it in their backyards. Is that also going to be child neglect? Just blind plea it. Judge isn't going to send anyone to prison over that."

"I may try it. I'm not sure how they are going to prove child neglect, but my client is in jail and wants out, so I'll see what he wants to do."

So many times, clients in jail plead guilty when they are not or when the State can't prove it because they need to get out of jail and get back to their lives. County jails are notoriously worse that prisons. All my clients tell me this. My repeat criminal clients that have been to prison before are always scheming and wanting to know how quickly they can get transferred from county to the Department of Corrections. The life of a defense attorney is often measured in small victories. I defend my clients and make sure that the State has proven or can prove its case. I try to get my clients the help that so many of them really need. I try to make them productive citizens again and give them hope that their lives can be better.

Another felony pre-trial docket down, and now to start preparing for those set for trial. Between now and the jury term, I have court every day. I also have the murder and attempted murder preliminary hearing coming up for Matt this next week. Law school teaches you mechanics, but not the reality of preparing for criminal jury trials. Prosecutors and defense lawyers must be prepared for several cases at a time and be ready to go with all of them on the first day because many times the case you prepared for the most will not be the one you end up trying. But now that this docket is over, I have just enough time for lunch and drive to another county for a divorce docket.

CHAPTER 6

I'm at the usual felony docket today and I have five guilty pleas to do, three revocation or probation violation hearings, and two not guilty pleas. I call for each of my clients to see who is on time: about half of them are. I signal my clients that are pleading not guilty to get in line. I start filling out the plea packets for the other ones. I call them up one by one and go over their constitutional rights. I can ask these questions in my sleep, I think.

"What is your full name? Address? Date of birth? Social security number? Age? Highest grade you completed in school? Can you read and write English? Have you ever been treated for a mental illness? Are you on any medications that affects your thinking? Have you been prescribed anything that you should be taking that you are not taking?"

Then, I go over the individual charges and what they could be facing if they took it to trial and lost. Then go over their constitutional rights. You understand that you have the right to have a lawyer? That you are presumed to be innocent? That you have the right to remain silent or to testify on your own behalf? That you have the right to see and hear all witnesses of the state? That you have the right to call your own witnesses and present evidence in your defense? That the State is required to prove your innocence beyond a reasonable doubt? That you have the right to a jury trial and all jurors would have to agree that you are guilty or you could have a bench trial if the State agreed and have the jury or a judge decide your punishment? You understand that by entering a guilty plea you are giving up all those rights?

The next set of questions is the part I dread the most because I feel like more people perjure themselves here. "Did you commit the crime you are charged with? Are you pleading guilty because you are guilty and for no other reason? Have you been forced, abused, mistreated, or promised anything to enter this plea? Are you doing this of your own free will?"

I put these clients in line one by one. Then, I try to negotiate with D.A.'s office on my revocation hearings. This first client, Bob Bowers, is a guy that was on probation for breaking into a car and has been arrested two more times for possession of methamphetamine, but he has listened to my advice and started outpatient treatment and on a waiting list for rehab. "Travis, can we set over sentencing to allow my guy to get into rehab? Here's a copy of his last 3 negative drug tests, AA meetings, and a letter from his drug and alcohol counselor."

"Lindsey, this guy had 3 priors before this one and this is his second revocation. He needs to do six months in jail."

"Six months in jail will not help him end the addiction cycle. You and I both know he can just as easily get drugs on the inside as he can on the outside. Even if he stays clean, jail won't teach him any coping mechanisms and when he finishes, he'll go right back and you know it," I argue my case to him.

"How long will it take for him to get into rehab?"

"A bed should be available in three weeks."

"Fine, he can do rehab if he sits in jail the next two weeks and then gets his affairs in order to go to rehab, but if he doesn't complete it for any reason, no more deals."

"I'll sell it to him. Next one: Raven Shields is on for failure to pay restitution, but she has paid $600 on it but lost her job which is why she didn't pay for two months. She has just started at Taco Bell, but she can't afford very much and pay her court costs and probation fees. She has $50 to pay on it today. Can we just stipulate she got behind and come back in three months?" "That's fine but she needs to pay every month until we come back, or she needs to sit out a sanction."

The next case I have is with another ADA so I find her, "Hey Kelli, this guy is talking to me about hearing satellites so

I'm asking for a competency evaluation and I think I may have an insanity defense coming. So I'm just going to ask for a review date. Does that work for you?"

"I think he's faking it so make sure you file a formal motion and set it for hearing if you are asking for the State to pay for this evaluation."

"Since he's incarcerated and has already been determined indigent, I'm sure he will qualify, but I will." I stop myself from rolling my eyes.

This docket took up most of my morning, but I have enough time to review my messages, sign documents, and give instructions to Lea on when to schedule appointments. She has made copies of all the documents I worked on last night, so I take them back across to the courthouse to file them and put copies in the opposing lawyer's boxes.

I walk upstairs and knock on my best friend Regan's office door. Regan is a court reporter on the domestic and juvenile docket. She opens the door. "Hey Lins, are you done with court?"

"I am for this morning anyway. Want to do lunch?"

"Sure, I can take a break from this transcription. Let's go." She smiles and shuts down her machine and grabs her purse.

We walk back across the street to my car and head to our favorite deli just around the corner to have a sandwich and salad and the best tea and cookies in the world, or so I think anyway.

"Did you report on anything interesting this morning?"

"Actually, someone requested a reporter for this protective order hearing. We aren't even finished. We are coming back again tomorrow. There is also a companion divorce proceeding. The wife claims that her husband put a gps tracker on her car or her phone because he continuously showing up wherever she is. But get this, they also work at the same place and she keeps going over to his mother's and brother's houses, but admits that she has been sleeping with her brother-in-law. She also says that he is also sending sexually explicit videos of her in bed with him and the brother-in-law to her from different numbers and even posted one of them on Snapchat, but of course, that's been deleted, and she can't prove it. His attorney continues to say but you can't prove he's sending them, right? She keeps getting hang up calls all hours of the day and night, but she also admits that her number was listed on a public dating site, but claims she didn't list it."

"At least you weren't bored. So what's new with you?"

She looks down and whispers. "I'm not sure I can keep this up with Chris. His outbursts are getting worse and worse."

"Regan, don't deal with that. If you are starting to fight come over to my place until he calms down. Is he willing to get any help, or do you think it is the pain pills?" I ask. They have a very up-and-down relationship. Chris and she got together five years ago, and things were good at first, but after the accident he hasn't been the same. When the truck hit him head on and broke his back, he's been on massive amounts of pain pills. He was a police officer and the force retired him and he is on disability. Since then, he abused her several times, but also is cruel and irritable. I'm sure there's a lot that she won't tell me, but I do know that she is madly in love with him. She's not one of those women that thinks she deserves it or that it's her fault, but she doesn't want to give up all the good with the bad.

"I've been begging him to go. He says he will, but then he always cancels at the last minute. I don't know what else to do. I'm walking on eggshells in my own home: worrying and waiting for the next explosion. I never know what will set him off. I love him and some days it's just like it always was, but other days, I dread going home. I almost hope that's he's asleep. Some of our best times now are when he needs me to take care of him. I just want my husband back. I rarely see him anymore."

"Maybe you need to set some clear boundaries and see a counselor yourself to help you deal with all this. I love you."

"Enough about me. Any interesting cases?"

"Yes, actually you'll be transcribing the preliminary hearing on the Flowers's murder and attempted murder case. He's a young kid. The victims were drug dealers. I think my client is actually innocent this time."

"I'll look forward to hearing that. We better get back before the afternoon docket.: She points at her watch. We pay the bill and head back to the courthouse for our afternoon dockets. *My boring marriage isn't so bad.*

This afternoon I'm scheduled on the juvenile deprived docket. This is a docket for cases when the Department of Human Services or child welfare has removed children from their parents. This could be for many reasons, such as domestic violence in the home, abuse of drugs or alcohol, or for more serious reason such as child abuse, molestation, or neglect. This is one of the more difficult dockets to handle because of the subject matter, but also because the lawyers almost have their hands tied because the outcome is mostly dependent on how hard your client works their program to get their children back. These are not cases where you can make some great argument and get a better deal or get your client out of the situation. This is an all or nothing system: either you have your children back in your custody or you don't. You have either gone to counseling or treatment or you haven't, except when you have done the plan and DHS still doesn't want you to have your kids back. Those situations are the most frustrating.

I sit through several cases where the parents feel the need to explain why they haven't gone to counseling or why they are still testing positive for drugs. They should let their attorneys speak for them, but for some reason on this docket, the clients seem to want to speak. One lady went on for ten minutes about all the things the Department was not doing, which are unacceptable, but two wrongs don't make a right. Regan and I share glances throughout the docket where I restrain from rolling my eyes. Then, I watch two dads relinquish their parental rights because their drug habit is more important to them than their children. Even if the children are better off with someone else, this is still sad because the children would still rather be at home with their parents.

Today, I have a father who has done absolutely everything he is supposed to do but the Department doesn't like him and

I'm furious. The stepchildren made allegations that he molested them, but I believe mom coached them to say that. No physical evidence and no corroboration. In fact, my client took an evaluation that the purpose is to see if he has a sexual attraction for children, and the evaluation showed absolutely nothing to indicate that and showed his urges as completely normal. He took a year of domestic violence classes. He has a good paying job. He has been in individual counseling for a year. He's married to a good woman, and they attend family counseling together. On the other hand, the mother has no job and recently went back to jail for failing to pay fines and is unable to take care of the children without state's assistance, but the Department still thinks she should have custody of my client's child because the siblings should stay together. In a perfect world that may be true, but there are multiple blended families in America and many siblings do not live in the same home.

    The judge finally recognizes the concerns we have been voicing and gives my client expanded visitation, but still leaves custody with the mother. My client and I will continue to fight this until we get into regular family court where I believe my client will win custody. Custody battles are one of the most common things that I handle, but also one of the most stressful. People are very emotional about their children, but also usually have a lot of hatred towards their ex and either intentionally or unconsciously use the children as weapons to punish their ex which only further harms the children.

CHAPTER 7

Today is an office day for a change. The first thing on the agenda is preparing for Matt's murder prelim. I've glanced through the reports before, but I'm really studying them today. The police narratives are the summary, but it references audio and video interviews that I do not have. The D.A. doesn't have to turn those over prior to preliminary hearing though. I flip to the summary and they interviewed Rachel in the hospital before she passed away.

Great. The D.A. is going to try to introduce her statements as a dying declaration. I'll have to research and file some motions, but I have one argument. She made this statement a few hours before she slipped into a coma, but three days prior to her death and she didn't know she was dying. The statement she gave supports her husband perfectly. Convenient they would have had plenty of time to get their stories together.

I highlight the relevant portions and get prepared to cross-examine Aaron if he testifies differently than his written statement. I will need those recordings before trial. I start research on dying declarations and gather as much relevant case law as I can and print the cases out in case, we have this argument tomorrow. The State may wait until trial for that.

I'm meeting Tyler, Will, and Micah for lunch. Our first topic of conversations is our interesting or troublesome cases. Tyler starts off, "So I have this lady who was a domestic violence victim and has completed everything DHS has asked her to do, but they still don't think she should get her kid back. They filed a motion to terminate."

"I have a couple similar cases. Maybe if we continue beating them at trial, this will change, but even when we win the trial, they can continue to deny returning them to their home. We have to have an ADA who is willing to stand up to DHS and not just go along with everything they say."

"If I become district attorney, I will put someone else in charge of those dockets who will exercise some independent judgment."

"That will be refreshing," Tyler says.

"I have a client that was pulled over for a traffic violation after the police admit to following him for a half mile. They were obviously waiting for a reason to pull them over. Then, police decide to impound the car and use that as a reason to search the vehicle and find a shotgun in the backseat. Four people in the car and they charge all four of them with the gun because all were felons." Micah explained.

"There's case law that says you cannot jointly possess a gun. It's not like drugs. People can divide drugs, but only one person can possess or use a gun at a time. Was there any proof of knowledge by all of the individuals?"

"No, but we are just at preliminary hearing stage now."

"This is a perfect example of a waste of resources and what I want to change with law enforcement. This is a waste of the court's time and taxpayer's dollars."

"I have a case set for trial where the cops beat my client up while they had barely a scratch on them and the State wants ten years in prison. The excessive force should count for some of the punishment."

"So ready for you to win and for us to have a change in the office. Not only are they being ridiculous with their offers, but half of them are just downright hateful," Tyler sighs.

I enjoy my lunch with them, finish a few more things up at the office, and review my messages Lea sent me throughout the day. "Lea, please call Anne and tell her I've sent a proposed decree of divorce to the opposing counsel."

"I hate to be the bearer of bad news, but this printer needs a new cartridge, and I'm having to order more postage from stamps.com."

"I'll order the ink if you can stop off and pick it up later. You can leave a few minutes early."

"Will you please get these cases set for mediation?"

"Yes, but I still haven't gotten a response on the ones I sent over last week," she tells me.

I grab my mail and write the payments down in the receipt book, then I walk back to the office to start my next pile of work. Mail usually brings more work: I received a response on a divorce. I received discovery requests on a case I have with Tyler. I also received copies of a docket from another county showing when my cases are set. I grab those files, write the dates on the files, and leave them out for Emily to file.

I text Emily, "Hey the filing is ready for you again. Tomorrow, I also need you to run some errands for me. I'll leave you post-it notes. You can use my truck. I'll leave the keys."

"Thanks, I will get on that and be there in the morning to pick up the truck and start on the errands. I'll file after I run the errands."

Emily is kind of a personal assistant as well. She does a variety of projects for me-mostly at work, but some things at home that I don't want to do or don't have time to do.

"Lea, I'm taking the rest of my work with me. I'm headed home so if you need me, you can reach me by phone."

"See you tomorrow."

CHAPTER 8

The day of Matt's prelim arrived. We are in a tiny courtroom with little space separating the prosecution and the defense tables and my clients always want to talk, but the prosecutors are not above eavesdropping. I always worry about that, so I hand Matt a legal pad and a pen and tell him, "Stay quiet, but write down anything you think when listening to the witnesses." He nodded in acknowledgment.

The prosecutor is a man named Robert Coyle: a cocky individual who thinks he is always on the right side and that police and "victims" never lie. He's gotten worse since he became First Assistant and now, he's running for district attorney against Will. The campaign has gotten nasty and divided the entire legal community. They continue to claim Will has no experience and can't do the job just because he's never been a prosecutor, but he's been an attorney for 15 years. He will be fine. Nevertheless, things are more tense than normal between the D.A.'s office and the defense bar that is supporting Will.

The presiding judge is the Honorable Jared Masterson. Judge Masterson has been on the bench for about fifteen years. He is one of the few judges that came from private practice and never worked for the D.A.'s office. He comes out and calls the case stating, "We are on the record in The State of Oklahoma v. Matthew Flowers. Please announce your appearances for the record."

"Robert Coyle for the State."

"Lindsey Jones for the Defense."

"State are you ready to proceed?"

"Yes, your Honor."

"Ms. Jones?"

"Yes, your Honor."

"State call your first witness."

"The State calls Aaron West.

The victim witness coordinator ushers him in. "Please raise your right hand."

West raises his hand. "Do you solemnly swear that the testimony you are about to give will be the truth and nothing but the truth?"

"I do."

"Please state your name for the record."

"Aaron West."

"I want to draw your attention back to May 17th of last year. Where were you?"

"I was at my home."

"Who was with you?"

"My girlfriend Rachel Graves, and then later James came over and brought the Defendant."

"By the defendant do you mean Matthew Flowers?"

"Yes."

"Can you point him out and describe what he is wearing?"

"Yeah he's sitting in the orange coveralls next to that lady lawyer."

"Your Honor, may the record reflect the identification of the Defendant?"

"It will so show.

"So Mr. West, had you ever met the Defendant before that night?"

"No that was the first time."

"What did he come over for?"

"Just to hang out." West avoids eye contact

"Were you friends with James? Had he been to your house before?"

"Yes we'd hung out a few times."

"What were you doing?"

"We were just hanging out."

"At some point did the night take an unusual turn?"

"Yeah, James received a phone call and said he had to go run an errand and would come back for Matt, which I thought was strange, but didn't make an issue of it."

"What happened next?"

"We were just hanging out at first then Matt swore that he heard a gunshot outside, so he and I went outside and didn't say anything. Then, he started tripping saying that people were coming after us and James may have brought people back to rob me. I kept telling him that we were fine and then he pulled his gun out and said, 'Y'all are setting me up, but I'm no punk. I won't go down without a fight,' and pointed his gun at me and shot me in the shoulder. I fell down and then I heard another gun shot and heard Rachel scream."

"So, you were shot in the shoulder, did you receive medical treatment?"

"Yes, I had to have surgery to remove the bullet. I still have some pain in that shoulder."

"How long were you in the hospital?"

"A few hours."

"What happened to Rachel?"

"She was shot in the stomach. After I got over the shock, I went over to her and tried to stop the bleeding, but it was so fast. I put my shirt over her and called 911."

"Where was the Defendant at this time?"

"He started running away and I chased after him. He fired back at me again and so I fired until I eventually saw him fall so, I figured I must have hit him, so I went back in to check on Rachel. She was barely breathing. I just tried to keep her calm." West starts to cry.

"Take your time and I'm sorry to ask, but what happened to Rachel?"

"She died three weeks later."

"So what happened between the shooting and her passing away?"

"The ambulance came, and then they worked on her until she got to the hospital. She had a couple surgeries and we all thought she was going to make it, but she got an infection and was too weak to recover."

"I know you've been through this, but for the record, who shot you?"

"The Defendant did."

"Who shot Rachel?"

"The defendant did."

"Do you know why?"

"I don't know. He was just so paranoid, but there was no reason at all for him to shoot us."

"No further questions."

Judge looks at me. "Ms. Jones, cross?"

"Yes, your honor." I march to the podium.

"Isn't it true that you were selling drugs to James and Matt that night?"

"Objection."

"Response?" Judge looks at me.

"This goes to the issue of credibility, Your Honor."

"Overruled, you may answer."

"No." West snarked.

"You were all smoking and shooting methamphetamine that night, weren't you?"

"No, we were just hanging out and talking."

"Can you explain why both you and Rachel had methamphetamine in your system according to your medical records?"

"How do you have my medical records?"

"Sir, you didn't answer my question can you explain why you had methamphetamine in your system when you went to the hospital?"

"No, I can't."

"Isn't it true that both you and Rachel had guns in your possession?"

"I always have my gun. Rachel didn't get hers until Matt and I went outside."

"Isn't it true that you pointed your gun at Matt first?"

"No, I didn't. Your client started saying we were out to get him and waving his gun around and then shot me for no reason."

"So, a person you had just met, shot you and your girlfriend for no reason?"

"I guess so."

"Are you a drug dealer sir?"

"No, I'm not, West responds.

"Aren't you charged with trafficking in methamphetamine?"

"Objection, your honor, relevance and improper impeachment."

"Your Honor, the witness opened the door by denying that he was a drug dealer and his use of methamphetamine, so it still relates to credibility."

"This isn't trial counsel, move along."

"Have you been offered any deals from the prosecution in regard to your testimony?"

"Objection!" Coyle shouts again.

"Overruled, this is a proper line of inquiry," Judge Masterson says.

"Not for my testimony," the witness says.

"Have you been offered anything at all by this prosecutor's office?"

"I've just been offered a suspended sentence on my pending case."

"You mean to trafficking methamphetamine?" I press.

"Yeah."

"Are you aware that trafficking in methamphetamine requires prison time and not probation?"

"Objection that calls for a legal conclusion."

Judge Masterson answers, "He can answer if he knows. Go ahead Mr. West."

"I don't know."

"Would it surprise you to learn that crime for which you cannot receive probation?"

"I guess."

"Why did you leave your girlfriend to chase after Mr. Flowers?"

"I was scared he might come back and try to finish us off."

"But didn't you testify earlier that he was running away?"

"Yes, but I wasn't sure if he was going to meet other people or what. I just wanted to protect Rachel."

"But wouldn't it have made more sense to stay with your girlfriend who had been shot?"

"I don't know maybe."

"When did you call 911?"

"After I got up and saw Rachel had been shot also."

"Why didn't you stay on the phone with them rather than running after Mr. Flowers?"

"Because the 911 operator just kept asking lots of questions and I heard noises outside and like I said I was afraid he would come back."

"Do you know where Mr. Flowers was shot?"

"No."

"If I told you he was shot in the back would you disagree?"

"I guess not."

"So, Mr. Flowers was in fact running away and not a danger to you when you shot him in the back isn't that true?"

"No, he was firing back at me."

"You haven't been charged with shooting Mr. Flowers, have you?"

"No, he shot us first. He killed my girlfriend for no reason."

"Yet Mr. Flowers was shot in the back several yards from the house?"

"Your Honor, may I have a moment to confer with my client?"

The judge nods and I walk back to the table. "He's lying Lindsey. Ask him about his security system and if it was recording."

"Mr. West did you have a security system at your home?"

"Yes."

"Did it record any footage from this night?"

"I don't know, the police took it, but it didn't always record."

"Did you have cameras inside the house?"

"No just outside to see if anyone is coming."

"No further questions."

"State, any redirect?"

"Not at this time."

Judge Masterson then says, "Let's take a ten-minute recess."

CHAPTER 9

We took a ten-minute break in which I ran to the bathroom and chatted with my client.

"We are back on the record, State, call your second witness."

"Your Honor, the State would offer the Medical Examiner's Report by stipulation." "Ms. Jones?"

"No objection for this hearing."

"Anything further State?"

"The State calls Deputy Goins."

Deputy Goins comes forward and the Judge swears him in.

Coyle starts with the preliminary questions, "Please state your name and occupation."

"Jason Goins, and I'm an investigator with the Sheriff's Office."

"Were you the investigator assigned to work a shooting on May 15, 2017?"

"Yes, anytime there is a shooting, the responding deputy calls for an investigator to come out."

"What did you see when you arrived on scene?"

"First, I saw a woman being transported into an ambulance. The other deputies told me she was severely injured. Then, I saw paramedics treating Aaron West. I also saw the paramedics putting Defendant Matthew Flowers on a stretcher. We had spotlights on because it was dark. I walked into the house and saw a lot of blood and I also noticed blood stains as I walked up towards the house."

"Did you speak to anyone at that time?"

"No, I asked the paramedics what hospital they were headed to and decided that I would wait until they were medically cleared to interview them."

"Did you interview the individuals at some point?"

"Yes, but I took some other steps in my investigation first so that I would know what was going on. I talked to the responding deputies and learned that the call came from Mr. West who said that the Defendant shot both. I also learned that Mr. West shot Mr. Flowers. Then, I applied for a search warrant for the West home so I could gather any evidence of guns, bullets, and any other evidence related to this case. A judge granted me the search warrant of the residence and I and some other deputies executed that search warrant."

"Objection the witness is launching into a narrative and not answering the questions."

"Sustained. Answer the question that is asked."

"When you say the Defendant, can you identify who you are talking about?"

"The man in orange coveralls seated next to Ms. Jones."

"Did you speak to this Defendant at some point?"

"Yes, I met him at the hospital the next day. He had surgery to remove a bullet, but he was awake and alert. I read him his Miranda warning at that point because we had an officer stationed in his room because we had him in investigative detention. He agreed to talk to me at that time."

"What did he tell you happened?"

"He said that Aaron said he heard what sounded like a gun shot outside and he and Aaron went outside to check it out but found nothing and that when they came back in Rachel had a gun with her. He said that Aaron then pulled a gun on him and threatened him and that he pulled his gun out and shot him. He then said Rachel aimed her gun at him and he shot her. Then he ran out and Aaron kept shooting at him until he was hit in the back, fell to the ground, and passed out at some point."

"So, the Defendant admitted to shooting both Aaron West and Rachel Thompson?"

"Yes, he did."

"Did you talk to Mr. West?"

"Yes, I took his statement after I took the Defendant's."

"What did he tell you?"

"Objection hearsay and cumulative as we just heard from Mr. West."

"Sustained."

"Were you able to talk to Ms. Thompson at that time as well?"

"No, I was not she was still in surgery fighting for her life."

"Were you ever able to speak with her?"

"Yes, about a week or so later, she was coherent enough for me to interview her."

"What did she tell you happened?"

"Objection hearsay."

"Your Honor I submit that this would be a dying declaration by Ms. Thompson which would be an exception to the hearsay rule."

"Your Honor, the prosecutor hasn't laid the foundation for a dying declaration. Further, Ms. Thompson didn't pass away for a few days so it could not be a dying declaration."

Judge Masterson then says, "I'm not going to hear this argument, I will leave this to the District Judge, but I am ending this preliminary as the State has met it's burden of probable cause for Count 1 Murder in the First Degree and Count 2 Shooting with Intent to Kill. Bond will remain $300,000 Ms. Jones when do you want your arraignment?"

"In two weeks, Your Honor."

"Anything else we need to address?"

The prosecutor and I both answer "No," and the judge leaves the bench.

"Matt, we'll be in touch. I'll be filing a Notice of our defense of self-defense. I'll see you at arraignment."

"Lindsey, how can he just lie like that?" Matt asks, looking a bit panicked.

"It happens, Matt but this wasn't going to be our hearing, this is just preliminary hearing. We won't get to present our side until trial. Hang in there. We've still got a lot of work ahead of us."

I turn to leave and see Glenda sitting in the gallery as she rises and comes towards me. "Lindsey, that wasn't good. What are you going to do?"

"Glenda, it never looks good for the Defendant at this point. I will order a transcript of this hearing and we will have his testimony on the record and if he deviates, I can impeach him at trial. Also, we learned that he is getting a deal. We've learned some things, but like I just told Matt, we have a long way to go. Don't lose hope!"

"I trust you. This is just so scary!"

"I know, Glenda, and I promise I will do everything I can to help your son."

After the preliminary hearing was over, I return to my office hoping I can grab my files and head home, but first I have multiple phone calls to return and mail to open and miscellaneous things to do. So, it's a little after five before I'm able to leave. When I get home, I see that Justin is already home. *Great, we can have an early nice dinner out.* When I walk in, I notice that there are candles lit, dimmed lights, and the table is set. I smell a delicious aroma of food. I walk into the kitchen and see Justin pulled some chicken out of the oven and see a whole meal prepared including salad, mashed potatoes, noodles, and garlic bread.

"Hey what got into you? This smells and looks great."

"I knew you had that murder hearing today so thought it might be a good night to relax."

"It's perfect. Thank you." I tell him and give him a kiss on the cheek and ask, "What do I need to do?" He never does this kind of thing, *I wonder what got into him, but I'm not going to complain.*

"Nothing unless you want to turn some music or something on. Just go have a seat at the table. I'll bring food out in just a minute. Do you want tea to drink?"

"Yes, thank you." I turn on a podcast that we've been listening to together and it plays through a Bluetooth speaker.

He comes in shortly carrying drinks for us and then returns with plates full of food and sits across from me.

"This is nice. Thank you, babe. I was going to suggest we go out and have a nice dinner, but this is even better."

"You're welcome. How did the hearing go?"

He's never interested so I launch into what happened. "Pretty well for a prelim. Their witness is not very believable, and the State is trying to act like they haven't offered him a deal, but he is getting probation on what was a trafficking charge. You can't get probation on trafficking, so they are amending to a lesser charge. They tried to introduce his deceased girlfriend's statements at the hospital. That's going to be a fight, but she made them two weeks before she passed away so I don't see how that can be a dying declaration. How was your day?"

"Oh, you know nothing exciting. Just preparing financial statements and reports and I finished early so came home around four."

We then eat listening to our podcast and I just enjoy the peace. After dinner, "Go on into the living room and find something for us to watch, I'll clean this up."

"Are you sure? There's a lot."

"Absolutely, the food was wonderful. It's the least I can do, but you can let the dogs back in."

Justin puts on the newest Netflix tv series for us to start to binge. I come in after putting the food and dishes away and join him on the couch. He looks at me. "No work tonight?"

"I brought some, but it can wait. I think I'll just enjoy a night with you." I say with a wink. He smiles at that and squeezes my hand. We sit there, hand in hand, like we haven't done in a long time. I'm not sure what has gotten into my husband, but it is nice for him to flirt with me again. We sit there like that for a while watching television. That night when we went to bed, we made love and it wasn't perfunctory. It was meaningful, and the best night's sleep I had in months.

CHAPTER 10

This Friday morning, I only have a couple of agreed divorce hearings and then I can work on the files I didn't last night. The first is a couple that has only been married for a few years and has no children, but surprisingly accumulated quite a bit of property. Even though the parties have come to an agreement, certain things must be put on the record, at least in this district. Judge Lori Oakes enters from her chambers and another attorney announces, "All rise."

Judge Oakes positions herself at the bench, "Thank you. You may be seated. Please turn your cell phones off. I will call the cases in the order they are printed in the docket. If the matter turns out to be contested, we will come back to it at the heel. Morris v. Morris."

That happens to be my case, so I rise and announce, "Present with counsel, may my client and I approach?"

"Yes. This matter comes on for final agreed divorce hearing correct?"

"Yes, Your Honor."

Judge Oaks looks to my client and swears her in. I ask her a series questions and her answers are yes. This ritual I find pointless when we swear to all of this and sign to it in pleadings. In other civil cases, you don't have to swear in before things are finalized if you have all signed an order.

"You were married to Richard Morris on April 24, 2016 in Oklahoma City, Oklahoma, and have lived together since the filing of this divorce? You are asking for a divorce on the grounds of incompatibility? There's hope that this marriage can be saved? You two had no children that are grown, you are not pregnant, and are not in the process of adopting a child correct? Has this decree divided all of your real and personal property and is it fair to both parties? You understand that you cannot remarry in the State of Oklahoma save and except back to Mr. Morris?"

"In Morris v. Morris, the decree of dissolution is approved, and divorce is granted. Ma'am you cannot remarry in the State of Oklahoma for the next six months. Counsel take and file with the court clerk. I signal for my client to follow me as I step into the hallway and down the hall to the Court Clerk's office to file the decree and get certified copies for her and the other side.

Judge Oakes has been working her way through the docket and as I wait for my next case, I look around the room and play "What not to wear" in my head. One lady is wearing miniskirt and high heel boots. One guy is in pajama pants. Another man wears shorts. Another man in a suit like an attorney. Those are the highlights anyway.

Then I hear the judge call my other case, "Johnson v. Johnson this comes on for Motion to Settle the Journal Entry. Ms. Jones, it's your motion, go ahead."

"Your Honor, I filed this because opposing counsel had not received permission from his client to sign the journal entry I prepared based on your ruling at the last hearing; however, this morning, counsel signed the journal entry and am ready to present it to you for signature."

"Very well." She takes the order from me and signs and hands back to me.

I feel my phone vibrate and receive a text from Regan that reads, "Do you and Justin want to come over tonight? Chris is going to grill some steaks and stuff."

I text her back and answer, "I don't think we had any plans, but let me check with him and I'll get right back to you but sounds great."

I text him and he says whatever I want to do so I text Regan back and ask what we can bring. Of course, she says nothing, but finally says a bottle of wine.

The rest of the day passes, and I stop off at a liquor store to pick up a nice red wine. I change out of lawyer clothes and change into clothes to go out in. When Justin gets home, he drives us in his Range Rover over to Regan's house a few blocks away.

On the drive Justin asks, "I thought Regan and Chris were having problems?"

"He is still losing his temper at her. She's trying to work on it."

I've been over to Regan's a lot more than Justin when we've had some girls' nights when Chris has been out of town, but Justin has been over enough to know Chris and feel comfortable. When we walk up to the house and Regan is already at the door, "Hey Lins, hey Justin. So glad you're here. Let me take your coats. Chris is out back finishing the steaks if you want to go join Justin."

Justin speaks first, "Thanks for having us. I'll head out back."

Regan and I go into the kitchen and finish setting the table and pouring glasses of tea and wine. "Your house looks great. Thanks for the invite. So are things better than last week?"

"He seems to be making more of an effort. I thought this would be good for us. How are things with Justin?"

"We had a really good night the other night. He had dinner cooking for me when I got home, and we relaxed and watched a movie cuddled on the couch. Seemed like old times you know. I feel happier than I have in a while."

Just then, I hear Chris say, "Ladies if you want to bring the plates and you can pick your steak."

"Great hon, we'll be right there."

We head out onto the back deck. "Smells and looks wonderful, Chris."

"Thanks, it's been a while since we've had people over. It's nice to have a reason to grill." He puts a steak, corn on the cob, baked potato on each plate. We all head into the dining room with our plates and Regan and I pour glasses of wine and tea for everyone. Chris and Justin follow in shortly behind us and sit down.

We chitchat about random topics, when Chris asks, "Lindsey, do you have any interesting cases going right now?"

"I have a murder and assault with a deadly weapon. Client shot his drug dealer and his girlfriend. Girlfriend died. May have a decent self-defense argument. Regan did the reporting on it the other day."

Chris got a weird look on his face and had a slight snarl. "I don't know how you stand to represent criminals all the time."

"Everyone is entitled to a defense." An awkward silence follows. Regan looks at me with an embarrassed expression. Thankfully, Justin saved the day and starts talking to Chris about sports. The rest of the evening goes well enough and then after the meal we had coffee and chocolate mousse cake.

REGAN

"That was fun tonight, Chris. I'm glad we had people over."

"I don't think you need to hang out with her. She represents dangerous people. She could be in danger anytime and that puts you at risk." Chris barks.

"She's just doing her job and I see all of those same people every day in the courthouse."

"She's trying to get a murderer off for self-defense. That should bother you."

"I don't feel like arguing. We've had a good night. Let's go watch a movie." *I hope he drops it.*

"I just think that guy is guilty. If he shot his drug dealer, he probably didn't want to pay and needed his drugs anyway."

"You may be right." I tell him, while resisting the urge to roll my eyes and head into the living room.

CHAPTER 11

I am sitting and waiting at the initial appearances docket waiting for my new DUI client's case to be called, when I hear the judge say, "Matthew Flowers, I have before me an information charging you with Conspiracy to Intimidate a State's Witness." I immediately perk up and move to the front of the courtroom where the judge is conducting video court.

"Ms. Jones, have you received a copy of the charges?"

"No, your Honor, this is the first I'm hearing of these charges, but I will accept them on his behalf and waive reading." I shake my head at the prosecutor who hands me the charges. It's not actually this prosecutor's fault. The newest lawyer in the office always handles initial appearances. Her name is Sheila Snider who just graduated law school and only handles misdemeanors. When I receive the paperwork, I see that Coyle signed these charges. He could have extended some professional courtesy and told me that these were coming.

"Mr. Flowers your attorney is present in the courtroom. Your next court date will be in two weeks. If she is not going to be your attorney, you can apply for court appointed counsel or hire counsel, but you will need an attorney. Ms. Jones, anything you want me to relay to your client?"

"Just that I will be out to see him and discuss the charges. May I have a copy of the probable cause affidavit?"

The Judge hands me a copy and says, "You can go in chambers and make a copy but please return my original."

I nod and head back to chamber reading a little bit while I'm walking. The complaining victim in our murder case was attacked at a local bar by a friend of Matt's and the attacker said, "This is for Matt."

Apparently, the attacker has been corresponding with my client while he has been locked up. This is a stretch. Just another way to try to scare my client into taking a plea.

I go back into the courtroom and hand the clerk back the Affidavit. Judge lets me handle my other client next. I'm still fuming over this new and ridiculous charge. After my other client leaves, I contemplate going to the district attorney's office, but I realize I'm not in the right state of mind and might say something I regret. Then I think, I need to notify Matt's mother of this new hiccup. I get back into my office and pull his file and find Glenda's number.

On the third ring she answers with, "Hello Lindsey, what's wrong?"

"Glenda, I hate to call with bad new but at court today, they arraigned Matt on new charges of Conspiracy to Intimidate a State's Witness."

"What?" She shrieks. "How could he intimidate someone in jail?"

"The charges appear to be ridiculous and very weak, but they are claiming a friend of his that has been in contact with him beat Aaron up at a bar and said, 'This is for Matt."

"Oh my gosh so what now?"

"I'll get the state's discovery and we'll have a preliminary hearing on this one too. I really think this is more about trying to scare him out of having a trial or make things harder on him. Try not to worry and we'll just keep going."

"Thank you for calling me."

"You're welcome. Try to have a decent day. I'll talk to you later."

I work in my office the rest of the day preparing motions, but I call Nick on my way home and he answers on the second ring, "Hey Lins, what's up?"

"You're never going to believe what Coyle filed now."

"What now?"

"You know about my murder defendant?" I say rhetorically (because we have talked about it more than once, so I know he does) and continue, "Coyle filed a new charge that I've never seen before, 'Conspiracy to Intimidate a State's Witness.' My client has been in jail this whole time. Can you believe that?"

"How and who did he conspire with? and what happened?"

We always have a levelheaded back and forth on our cases, which is why we run our stuff past each other. I fill him in on the details.

"To get a conspiracy they are going to have to prove an agreement. If they don't have anything at prelim, I think Clarkson would kick it out, but why do you think they filed. I mean this is small potatoes compared to murder."

"I'm guessing they are going to file a Burk's notice and try to admit this in the murder trial as evidence of guilt."

"I think that's an easy win on a motion in limine for you. He's also doing it to screw with you and look tough in this campaign. I've got a case to tell you about. I've got a guy who has been caught with a pound of what turned out to be rock salt and they are still wanting to send him to prison on felony attempting to traffic drugs. I'll just take that to trial."

"That's just dumb. Is that Coyle as well? I wish the voters

knew this is how he is wasting the taxpayer's dollars. I've got to go headed home to change and then to work the county fair with Will tonight."

I get to the fair and Will and his wife and two of his daughters are with us. Two booths down are the Coyle campaign and he and several employees of the D.A.'s office are there as well. Coyle has a much bigger pool of volunteers to draw from because there are forty employees that work for the D.A. We are mostly solo practitioners. But here we are just waiting to talk to people and answer questions if they have any. Most just want to get our candy or water or balloons. I'm so tired of tying balloons I could scream! I never knew how difficult blowing balloons was. My fingers are chapped and blue.

We are sitting handing out our stuff when an older man gets to our booth, "I just talked to the other guy, why should I vote for you?"

Will steps out to talk to him, "I want to make our community safer by focusing on violent crime and getting addicts and the mentally ill the help they need so they don't victimize the community anymore. We can't just keep locking everyone up and expecting them to come out and do anything differently without education and treatment."

"That makes sense. You have my vote and I see that you are a Republican, so I guess the other guy is a Democrat. Funny none of his material says that! Seems shady. Good luck."

We continue talking to people and blowing balloons until the place closes. It's been a long day, so I finally head home around 8:30. Justin starts in as soon as I walk in the door. "Nice of you to finally come home."

"I told you we had to work the fair tonight. You could have come out and helped."

"It's like you have a second job with this campaign, but it's not bringing in more money." He just wants to fight.

"You know why I'm helping him. First, on principal, we need to stop dehumanizing people and just considering them criminals and throwing people in prison. A lot of the people I deal with either made a mistake or are sick. You know the current D.A.'s office doesn't get that. Second of all, it will be a boost to my business because I would have a better relationship with the new D.A. and make my life easier instead of trying so many cases that don't need to be tried," I explain for at least the tenth time.

"Whatever you need to do to get attention and get people to like you and see how great you are."

I sigh. "Justin, I've had a long day. I don't know why you are wanting to fight, but I'm tired and don't feel like fighting with you." With that, I walk past him to the bedroom to get in pajamas and relax and watch some tv. I really wish he understood me or cared about my causes or any causes really. He doesn't get passionate or involved in anything for the community.

CHAPTER 12

When I arrive at the office, I realize that I left Matt's file at home. Like Nick and I predicted, the State did file a Burk's notice to bring in this "alleged intimidation" incident. I finished my response last night, as well as filed a motion in limine to attempt to keep out the dying declaration that is a full interview. I need to get those filed today. *Oh, I'll just go get it at lunch.*

I head to the library where I am due for a mediation of a divorce that I don't think is going to settle because both clients are pretty hardheaded, but maybe if we separate and want to be reasonable. I don't like to go to mediation if I can avoid it, but honestly sometimes it is better if an attorney is there to try to bring some reason into what each person might get. I prefer when the mediator is an attorney who can back up what I am telling my client-even if they don't like it! I like my criminal cases the best, but honestly most of them don't have money. Divorces and custody battles help pay the bills.

The parties in this case have both filed for protective orders on the other and truthfully neither of them needs a protective order. They are just angry exes, but neither is danger nor has any real threat been made, but it's too easy to get one. It's one dirty trick that some divorce lawyers encourage you their clients to file for a protective order against their spouse and include the children so their spouse can't see them and gives you an upper hand in the divorce. These people were only married three years, but my client in his infinite wisdom added his wife's name to the deed to his home and five acres that he owned for twenty years prior to marriage. The wife, of course, now wants a huge amount of money to sign over the property. They also bought two vehicles and own some cattle and bought new furniture and other property. The wife quit her job once they got married and wants alimony because she has no income.

My client and I arrive first. Next the mediator comes in and says as he shakes our hands, "Hi I'm Carl. I'm the mediator today." We make our introductions and the attorney and other party Melissa come in.

He reads through all the mediation rules and I tune out during that as usual. He tells them that mediation is confidential and that nothing you say can be used against you later. If statements made during settlement negotiations were able to be used against you, we would never get anywhere. The mediators also explain that you are there talk to him and see if you can come to an agreement and not talk to each other. He starts with Melissa, "What are you looking to get out of this mediation?"

Melissa takes a breath and launches into it, "I want to get divorced, and I want him to leave me alone for good. I want what's fair. I sold my home and quit my job to marry him and stay home and be available to him and he cheated on me. I want alimony. I deserve that after what I went through with him. If he wants me off the deed to the home, he needs to pay me half of the appraised value. I want him to pay my car off. He needs to take the credit card debt. There are also several things in the home that I want. I also want my portion of his retirement. I also want our dog Zeus."

Carl writes it all down. "So you are wanting alimony, money instead of the house, him to pay for your car, and some furniture and things from the house, as well as the dog? Is that right?" Then, he turns to Joe and asks him what he wants.

"I want to get this divorce settled and done. I want her off the deed to my house that I have paid off and have had for twenty years, but just refinanced to remodel the home to make her happy. I didn't tell her to quit her job. She did that on her own because she wanted to do volunteer work and oversee the remodel of the house. She failed to mention that she also had an ongoing affair with the contractor. I only had a one-night stand..."

Melissa cuts in just then, "I did not! You're just overly jealous."

"Now let's just talk to me. I do know this is a no-fault divorce state, so blaming isn't going to help us." Carl signals for Joe to continue.

"I'm not paying her alimony, and I don't want her to touch my retirement. She's the one that used the credit cards and ran up about $5,000 in debt. She needs to get a job and pay her own car payments and her own credit cards that are in her name. She can take what she wants of the furniture and stuff, but she is not getting Zeus. It was my idea to buy him. I've been training him. He's my dog!"

He suggests that we separate and caucus. "To take turns, I'll move in there with them for a minute and try to get some more specific proposals and see where we can maybe reach some agreements."

Joe is huffy. "Joe, it's ok. It will be better separated like this and maybe we can get this resolved."

"Not if she wants to take my dog! I won't give in on that one."

"Do you think she really wants the dog or is using it as a bargaining chip?"

He sighs, "She loves the dog, but he's my dog. He follows me around, sleeps with me, and trains with me. I'm going to show him. He's comes from a champion bully line."

"Let's see where we get. If not, we'll go to trial. She left the house without the dog, so that would weigh somewhat in our favor."

Carl comes back in after about twenty minutes, which seems like an endless time when stuck in a room where you can't do much of anything. Carl explains their formal offer, "Melissa wants $1,000 a month for the next two years in alimony as well as $15,000. Once she receives the lump sum, she will sign a quit claim deed to you on the house. She will leave your retirement alone. She wants you to pay for her car and split the credit card debt. She wants the furniture-bedroom suit, appliances, two televisions, the Apple TV, end tables, china, and the couch. She also wants Zeus."

"Zeus is a deal breaker. I will not give her Zeus!"

"We can table that subject for now. What about the other stuff?"

"The money requests seem extreme when only married for three years. She is also a teacher and is perfectly capable of getting a job and earning money. If she wants money, then Joe isn't also going to pay off the car or her credit cards. The furniture stuff is fine. Joe, what's an amount you would pay her essentially to go away and get this done?"

"I'll pay her $10,000 for everything. No more claims on anything. Deal expires today and she would be paid within forty-eight hours. I also get Zeus."

When he leaves the room to take our counteroffer, "This is why I like to be separate for mediation because if you two were arguing in the same room you would both continue to be irritated and we would get nowhere."

Carl returns about ten minutes later.. "We are making progress. If she can get a lump sum of $25,000 within forty-eight hours, she will waive the house, car, retirement, and assume the credit card debt."

"What about Zeus?"

"She still wants him."

"Then no deal on any of it. If she wants money, then I get Zeus. Period. And she needs to decide today!"

"What about the $25,000? Are you willing to pay that much?"

"No I don't want to pay her that much. What do you think a judge might do if we went to trial?"

"The problem is that you did add her name to the house, and it increased in value because of the remodel. Her equitable division of that is unclear. This judge does tend to give some alimony. I don't know that he would give it for two years. I still think we are close and on the right track. How about offering $15,000?"

Carl comes back again. "$20,000 and I think we have a deal."

"I get Zeus?"

"Yes," Carl replies.

"What do you think?" Joe looks at me.

"It will get it done, but it's ultimately up to you. It's your money."

"Let's get this done. Are we going to sign something today? I don't want her backing out or changing her mind."

"You can all sign on the agreement I write up. I'll bring them back in so we can see the agreement and sign."

That one's done. I check my messages at the office and head home. When I pull in the driveway, I see Justin's car. *Huh he must have come home for lunch. He rarely does that.* I unlock the door. "Justin?" Then, I walk in and freeze. I can't believe what I'm seeing.

My assistant Emily is half dressed and on top of Justin on my couch. Now that I take in the room, I see clothes scattered about the room. I am stunned and paralyzed.

Emily shrieks, "Oh my god."

Justin jumps up throwing Emily off as she starts grabbing clothes trying to get dressed.

I'm still standing there not knowing what to do. I know Justin is trying to talk to me but it's like I'm in a fog. "Lindsey, I'm sorry..." as Justin tries to say the words, I put my hand up and walk past him into the bedroom. I'm so furious and hurt at the same time. I feel tears in my eyes, but they won't come out, but I know one thing: Justin needs to leave. Operating on instinct, I pull open the closet door and grab a large duffel bag. I go to the dresser and I start throwing his boxer briefs, socks, t-shirts in there. I go into the master bathroom and start throwing his toothbrush, his razor, and all his hygiene products in there. I'm on a mission.

Justin is follows me and keeps yammering. "What are you doing?" "Lindsey calm down." "Don't do this."

I just keep going. I go to the hall closet and get a suitcase. I head back to the master closet and start throwing some of his clothes and shoes in the suitcase. He's only a couple feet from me. I can tell wanting and trying to stop me but then he grabs my arm and I twirl around and scream, "DON'T YOU DARE TOUCH ME!"

He jumped back immediately and whispered, "I'm sorry."

"Get out." I look him straight in the eyes and say it without emotion.

"Lindsey, we need to talk."

"No, I don't want to talk to you. I don't want to see you. Just get out!" I shout at him and stare at him and I know I'm about to break down in tears. "NOW!"

He grabs the duffel bag and the suitcase, and the front door closes. I slide to the ground then and put my face in my hands and begin to sob. I don't know what to think. Justin is having an affair and with Emily? They have only met for a couple times at the house. I didn't even know they'd ever had a conversation. *They've had more than a conversation, stupid.* I sat there for a while when I hear the text message alert on my phone and look down and I see it's Justin, which I ignore, but I realize it's 1:05 and I'm clearly in no shape to go to court.

I text Mariah, "I can't talk or explain now, but I can't come to the docket. I have two people on the docket just for reviews on their domestic violence classes. Can you please cover for me?"

I hold the phone waiting for an answer hoping and praying she answers so I don't have to go in. My phone vibrates in my hand and she answers, "Of course. I hope you're ok. I'll talk to you soon."

I push myself up on the floor. I feel like I weigh a thousand pounds, but I manage to crawl on top of the bed and just bury my head in the pillow. I lay there for a couple of hours and then I decide I'm going to find out more about this affair. I go into my office and login to my AT&T account. I pull up Justin's phone and pull up the last month's text messages. I pull up Emily's number on my phone and I start cross referencing. Text messages are going back and forth that month, so I go back another month. The texting started about six weeks ago. The messages are sporadic, but they have been regularly communicating. It also appears that several of the messages are mms or multimedia messages. *Probably pictures or videos. Oh no! They may have been sexting.*

How did I miss this? I check the date of the first text message. I think back and pull up my calendar trying to think about what was going on. That week I let Emily drive our extra car to run errands. She must have seen him at the house and what? They just end up in bed. How does that even happen? How does my assistant end up in bed with my husband? Then it hits me, that dinner...it was guilt.

Here, I was thinking our marriage was getting stronger and really, he was just feeling guilty for screwing someone else. I feel sick: my stomach churns and feel nauseated. I want to talk to someone, but I don't. I don't even want to voice this out loud. My cat Lucy jumps in my lap then and as I rub on her, "At least I have you. My babies are loyal." I print out the phone records and let the dogs in.

I change into the pajamas and lay back on my bed and turn on the tv, but I have no idea what the programs are about. My phone is ringing, and I see it's Regan. "Hello, can you come over?"

"What's wrong Lins, you sound terrible?"

"I found Justin having sex with Emily on my couch today."

"I'll be right there."

A few minutes later, she comes in and hands me my keys that I hadn't bothered to take out of the door. I collapsed into her and just cried. She stayed with me for a couple hours. I told her everything I knew so far.

"I wonder what he was thinking," Regan muses aloud. "Do you want a divorce?"

"I don't know. I'm too upset to really think right now. I don't even want to see him right now. I mean we had drifted apart, but I thought we both took our vows seriously. Regan, I'll let you get home. Thank you for coming over."

"Anytime. You've always been there for me. Call me if you need me."

I walk her to the door and just stand there and decide to check my phone. There are twenty messages from Justin and three missed calls. I just can't deal right now. I went and found some nausea medicine that I have that puts me to sleep and set my alarm and head to bed. "Cinder, Dallas, Ricky, Lucy, come on let's go to bed," I call out to my babies.

CHAPTER 13

REGAN

I think about Lindsey and what she is going through when she walks through the door and hears, "Where the hell have you been? Do you know what time it is?" Chris screams at me while simultaneously walking me straight back against the wall.

"I texted you that Lindsey needed me. She caught Justin cheating on her. I was just over there comforting her. I'm sorry I'm late."

"Bullshit! Where were you really?"

"I was at Lindsey's. Call her and ask her if you don't believe me," she pleads for him to believe her, but his face is inches away, his fists clenched, and his whole body taut like he's ready to punch something. He is seething angry for no reason.

"It's 7:30. You are always home by 5:30. That's 2 hours. I tried to call you and text you with no response. What the hell am I supposed to think?" He backs away a little bit. "Where is your phone? Why didn't you answer?"

As I pull it out of my jacket pocket, I see ten missed calls and fifteen text messages. Before I can even open it, he snatches it out of my hand. "I'm going to see what you've really been up to."

"I must have forgotten to turn it off silent. I'm sorry. Go ahead and look. There is nothing on there."

"I'm hungry. Go get me something to eat."

I don't argue or it will get worse knows better. "What are you hungry for?"

He's deep in process of going through my phone. "Chris, can I have my phone so I can call in some food and go get it?" She begs.

He glares at me. "I still don't believe you. Just go get some Little Caesar's and some crazy bread."

I'm tired, but also hungry. I hate these moods of his and he didn't use to be like this, but this last year he has started exploding out of nowhere. Little Caesars is just a few blocks away and thankfully they aren't busy, so I'm able to get in and out and drive back home. When I return he's watching television in the living room, so I take it into the living room and set it down.

"What do you want to drink?" I walk into the kitchen to get plates, napkins, and drinks.

"Sweet tea." He answers without looking at me. I pour two glasses and takes the plates and napkins into the living room. "I don't need the plate, but thanks for the drink." Hyde has left and Jekyll has returned.

I relax a bit and eats a couple slices of pizza. He's watching "Impractical Jokers," so I'm watching it too. It's funny albeit in a stupid way, but he loves it. After a while he says, "Let's go to bed."

I pray that he will not want to have sex. I'm drained from that incident earlier and from helping Lindsey and not in the mood, but knows he often wants to have sex after a fight. When I get into bed, I turn the other direction, hoping he takes that as a sign and breathes a sigh of relief when he takes a shower before coming to bed.

I hate this, but I just can't imagine my life without him because I love him so much and he's my world.

CHAPTER 14

I hear a beeping noise—I thought was in my dream—when I finally realize it's my alarm. I roll over and see it's 6 A.M. I try to open my eyes enough to see what's on my calendar for today. I can't even remember. I don't have anything set. Thank you, Lord, I think to myself. Of course, He knew this was going to happen. I reset the alarm for 8 A.M. and go back to sleep.

When 8 o'clock rolls around, I turn the television on, feed my animals, and get a glass of juice and sit back up in my bed. I have a pounding headache and do not want to go into the office at all today, but I have paperwork that needs to be filed and mailed. I need to check my box because I'm waiting on some orders from Judge Kirby. Well that doesn't mean I have to go in this morning.

I've gotten several more missed text messages from Justin. I decide to finally read them. "Lindsey, I'm so sorry." "Please don't hate me." "It'll never happen again." "We've been together for years. Don't give up on me because I made a mistake." "Are you ok?" "Do you want a divorce?" "I'm sorry." "It didn't mean anything." "I was just being stupid." The messages continue and on in the similar vein. The same excuses everyone who has an affair has. I keep seeing them. It's like it's seared into my brain.

I decide to call my mom and see what she says. She answers on the first ring, "Hello? What are you doing?" I'm sure she is surprised I'm calling this early because I know she isn't a morning person.

"I'm at home. Yesterday I walked in on Justin having sex

with Emily."

"What? How did that happen? Start from the beginning."

"I came home at lunchtime to get a file I forgot, and there they were on the couch. Clothes strewn about. I just froze there in place for a minute. Emily just screamed and jumped up throwing on clothes and ran out the door. Justin was immediately trying to talk to me. I packed up clothes and personal stuff and told him to get out. He's been calling and texting almost non-stop."

"I'm so surprised by this. Have y'all been having problems?"

"Are you saying this is my fault? As if things weren't perfect it's ok to cheat?"

"Of course not. I was just asking is all. So, did he move out? Do you want a divorce?"

"No, he only left because I demanded it. I packed a few days' worth of stuff. He'll have to come back at some point to get stuff. I just couldn't bear to see him and needed to be alone."

"Why didn't you call me?"

"I just couldn't talk about it. Regan happened to call and came over for a while after work. I couldn't go to court. I was grateful Mariah was able to cover for me."

"I'm so sorry, honey. Do you need anything?"

"Unfortunately, I don't think there's anything you can do for me. I've just got to deal with it. I'm going to force myself to go to work for a while anyway."

"Yes, keep busy and don't talk to him until you're ready to do it. I love you."

"Love you too Mom. Going to go take a long hot shower. Goodbye."

I just stand there for a moment and lean against the wall with my eyes closed trying to think of how I'm going to keep going. As the water hits me, I decide that I'm going to go into work. I'm not going to let him get me down. I may not do much, but I'm not going to sit home and wallow.

I get into the office about 9:30 which is later than usual, but not too outrageous, so Lea doesn't think too much about it until she looks at me and says, "Lindsey, are you ok? You don't look too good."

"I've been better, Lea. Hold my calls, I just want to get some work done in my office," I tell her as I close the door to my office. I know I have stuff that I need to do but I can't process where to start, so I just sit there in the quiet for a little while. I finally grab a file and start working. Anything to take my mind off the hell that is going through my mind. I get up and go to the courthouse to check my box for orders I've been waiting on. I hear my name being called, "Lindsey, Lindsey!"

I look to see where the voice is coming from and a guy runs up to me and says, "You're Lindsey right?"

"Yes, I am can I help you?"

"I want to hire you for my case. I have court next month. I caught a possession with intent charge, but I wasn't selling," the guy says and then asks, "what's it gonna cost me?"

"$2500. Call my office to set something up." T try to keep walking, but he stops me.

"Will you take payments because I just paid my bondsman to get out and I was off work for a couple weeks, but I promise I got you."

"With a large down-payment and weekly payments, just call my office."

I have these conversations all the time. I started charging

consultation fees to see who was serious and who wasn't. Everybody has a story-a con that they have perfected. I go to lunch alone and read a book just to escape my world for a bit and because I can't stand to see anyone right now. I work for a couple more hours and head back home and get into lounging clothes and sink down in my oversized chair. I can't sit on my couch because I can still see Justin and Emily going at it.

I hear Justin's car pulling up in the driveway. *Great.* "Lindsey, we need to talk." He crouches down in front of me.

My pulse is skyrocketing in my chest. I can't help but glare at him. "There's nothing to talk about Justin. You cheated on me. You screwed my assistant on our couch in our home. What could you possibly have to say?"

"I'm sorry, Lindsey. It was just sex. I don't love her. If you want me to leave and never see me again then say so, but we can get past this." He tries to grab my hands and I turn away.

"I don't want to see you. That special night we had a few weeks ago, that was because you were feeling guilty wasn't it? How many times have you two had sex? Did you have sex in our bed? How did it start? Who made the first move?" My voice climbs in pitch and volume. "You want to talk? Then talk give me all the dirty details. Start by being honest if you still remember what that means!"

He backs up to the front door. "This was a mistake. You aren't ready to talk about this."

"No, you wanted to talk, so talk. What you just wanted me to say oh it's ok, let's pretend nothing ever happened. I don't think so!" I follow after him.

"I'm not going to do this with you." He then changes direction, lets the dogs in, and starts petting them. "Hey guys, did you miss me? Come here."

"You're the one that came home Justin. I just wanted

some peace and some time to deal with this, but no you're here wanting to talk; yet you don't want to hear what I have to say or answer any questions. Until you do, there is no reason for you to come home!" I

"Lindsey, it is a waste of money to stay at a hotel where am I supposed to go? This is my home too."

"You should have thought about that! Go to your mother's. Stay with a friend. Hell, go to Emily's for all I care." If I show anger, he won't see how hurt I am.

"I'm not going to Emily's. It was just a fling. It only happened a few times. I'm not staying with mom either she'll ask too many questions."

I cut him off. "Of course not, can't disappoint Momma. She would never believe her little boy isn't perfect."

"No need for the sarcasm, Lindsey. Fine I'll find somewhere else to stay for a couple days, but we can't do this forever."

"Forever, I found out yesterday and it wouldn't have ended but for the fact that I found out and how do I even know that it ended for that matter?"

"Of course, it's over. It was stupid."

"Just go." I'm emotionally exhausted, but at least he leaves. I sink back down in my chair and cry.

CHAPTER 15

At one of the usual preliminary hearing conference dockets I receive offers from the prosecutors and out of my seven clients, five of the offers were prison time. One said blind plea (let the judge decide sentence) or trial. One was life. This would be why we must have a change in the D.A.'s office. People think all of us criminal defense lawyers are bleeding heart liberals that are soft on crime, but we can understand prison for violent offenders, but first-time offenders that made a stupid mistake or someone with a substance abuse issue doesn't need to be caged like an animal. Tagging someone with a felony conviction ruins their life.

"Robert, are we abandoning the negotiations process now or what? I can't do anything with these offers but set them for hearing?"

"You all think I'm such an asshole, I might as well earn my reputation." He smirks at me.

I make my announcements to the Judge. "Miss Jones, is there a reason we are setting all of these cases for hearing?"

"Actually, yes judge all are prison offers, the State can't tell me if they have cooperating victims, one case there is no offer, and one the offer is life, so I really have no choice." I smile at Coyle enjoying that I threw him under the buss.

"I guess, nothing to lose then, but State maybe you prioritize if you are going to continue to file this many case, my docket is clogged as it is."

Before I leave, Coyle hands me a Burks motion to introduce the intimidating a witness charge in Matt's murder trial and motion to allow the deceased's statements in as a dying declaration. I'm not surprised, but now I'll respond. I need to watch the victim's interview in the hospital again and go over all the pictures on the CDs they sent. At least I have something to focus on and keep me busy this weekend.

I run upstairs to see Regan. "Lindsey, I'm so glad you stopped by. How are you?"

"I'm hanging in there. How about things with you?"

"Living the dream. Chris is who he is you know. Have you and Justin talked any?" I notice a bruise on her arm and for the second time today, my blood boils.

"He came home yesterday but we just had a screaming match and I had him leave again. I'm too upset to talk to him. I've got to get rid of that couch. I think I'm going to sell it on Facebook. I can't bear to look at it."

She chuckles. "I'm sorry it's not funny, but I'm just imagining if anyone asks why you are selling it what you would say." I can't help but smile. You must find the humor in everything.

"You going to tell me about that bruise?"

"I just bumped it on the counter."

I shake my head at her, so she knows I don't believe her." I'll let you get back to it. I've got some consultations scheduled this afternoon. Thanks for always being there." I say as I give her a hug and head out the door. As I pull away, I notice another bruise on the side of her neck.

"You know if you ever need to escape, my door is always open, and I can come get you anytime. No matter what."

"I know. Thanks."

I used to think there was something wrong if a woman stayed with a man that abused her, but the world isn't so black and white. There are many shades of gray and things are much more complicated than you realize. Just as I get settled back in my office and ready for my appointments, the door opens, and I assume it's Lea bringing me an intake sheet when I see Emily come in.

I inhale a quick breath and she starts yammering away, "Lindsey, look I'm so sorry. Let me explain. It's not Justin's fault. I came on to him. I was jealous and just wanted what you had. He didn't care about me."

"Just stop. I don't want to hear it. I think it goes without saying that you're fired. I don't know what I did to you for you to betray me like that, but I hope you can sleep at night. I'll write you your last paycheck." I pull the checkbook out, scribble a check and hold it out towards her.

"Lindsey, for what it's worth, thank you for this job and I am sorry."

She starts to leave. "Emily, I need all of my keys back."

"Right." She pulls the keys off one by one and exits. I exhale. Lea comes in the office and shuts the door. "Lins, I hate to pry, but what's going on? You don't seem yourself. Emily just said goodbye."

"I might as well tell you. I found Justin and Emily going at it on my couch a couple days ago."

"You're kidding me. I'm so sorry. Are you ok? Of course you're not ok. That's a stupid question."

"I'm taking it a day at a time. Do I have any appointments here yet?" I ask hoping to change the subject.

"No, they haven't shown up yet. Let me know if you need anything." She gives me a hug.

About half of my appointments show up that afternoon, and I gather up my files and head on home when Mom calls.

"Hey Lins, where are you?"

"I'm heading home. Your aunt Cathy and I are going to meet you there. We have some stuff for you."

That makes me smile. No matter how old I am, they always try to do special things for me.

Mom and Cathy bring up a home cooked dinner, a bag of my favorite Reese's peanut butter cups, and a twelve pack of Dr. Pepper. "We thought this might help you a bit."

"What's he saying?"

"He's been trying to apologize, but I'm not ready to talk to him. Emily came to the office today and I fired her. She tried taking the blame for it saying she came on to him, but he didn't have to reciprocate."

"Where's he staying?"

"He stayed at the La Quinta the first couple nights and was griping about the costs. I imagine he'll come by today because he'll need more clothes. I don't know what' I'm going to do."

"If you let him get away with it once, he'll just do it again."

"I know, but I'm not sure I want a divorce either, but I don't want to be around him now, so I don't know."

"I'd like to give him a piece of my mind." Cathy hisses.

After they leave, I change into pajamas. I'm too emotionally drained to deal with anymore.

Justin knocks and comes in, "Lindsey, I'm here."

I look up and nod at him. I go back to reading a book to forget about my world. He goes into the bedroom with his suitcase and duffel bag with him.

I call out to him, "What are you doing? I don't want you back home."

"I need to do laundry, and I'm not going to live in a hotel. This is my home too."

"You lost the right to share a bedroom with me by sleeping with someone else."

"I'm not moving out, and you can't make me."

"Actually, I could by filing divorce and getting exclusive possession of the house, but fine, if you want to make us both miserable move your things into the guest bedroom."

"Lindsey, this is ridiculous. Are we not even going to try to work this out?"

"I don't know, but I know I'm not sharing a bedroom with someone I can't stand the sight of right now, so take it or leave it."

He starts moving stuff into the other bedroom. There's a bathroom off that bedroom too. I go into the kitchen to heat up the meal Mom brought over and sit at the dining room table to eat it. Justin follows me. "Did your mom make that? Guess she hates me."

"She's not your biggest fan." He goes back into the kitchen and makes a sandwich and sits across the table from me. I get up and take my food into the living room.

"Really?"

"I'm not going to sit and pretend everything is fine. I told you I didn't want you here, but if you're going to be here, then do me the courtesy of avoiding me."

The food is delicious. Some of my comfort food-ranch chicken, mashed potatoes and gravy, corn, and rolls. I try to simply enjoy that and ignore that Justin is in the other room.

I text Regan, "He came home and is going to live in the guest room for now. I wish he would just move in with his mom or something for a while, but he won't leave."

"Are you ok?"

"I don't feel comfortable in my own home."

"I'm sorry girl. That feeling sucks.

REGAN

"Why don't you at least have the common decency to not be texting your boyfriend in front of me?"

"I'm texting Lindsey. Justin came home and is living in the guest room."

"I don't care. You're gone all day. You would think when you're home with me you would at least pay attention to me."

"I'm sorry. I'm done texting anyway. Dinner should be about done." I head into the kitchen trying to distract him.

"Let me see your phone." He grabs it out of my hand.

"Chris, there's nothing on there, so go ahead." After I pull the garlic bread out of the oven, I drain the spaghetti and mix in the meat and sauce.

"What's this crap about you understand not feeling comfortable in your own home? Are you talking about me? You don't talk about me or about us. What happens in our home stays in our home? Do you understand me?" He screams pinning me up against the counter.

"I didn't say it she did." *I must be more careful with texts. Even innocent comments he finds nefarious.*

"What are you saying about me?"

"We just talk about our marriages. That's what friends do. No big deal."

"Don't talk about me. Don't talk about us. It's no one's business. Do you understand me?" He squeezes my face.

"Yes. I'm sorry. It won't happen again."

He releases me after a couple minutes. "Hurry up and finish dinner. I'm hungry." He drops my phone on the counter.

CHAPTER 16

Finally, Judge Marshall Benson is going to rule on the motions in Matt's case. Judge Benson is particularly young for a district judge. He worked in the district attorney's office prior to taking the bench as a special judge and then being elected as district judge. He's very polite but tends to rule in the favor of the district attorney's office.

"We are here in the case of the State v. Matthew Flowers for ruling on pre-trial motions. State is present by First Assistant Coyle and Defendant is present in person and with counsel Lindsey Jones. State, it's your Burks motion, please explain why this other bad act should be allowed."

"Your Honor, the Defendant is charged with murder and assault and battery with a deadly weapon. One of his victims is Aaron West. Mr. West was enjoying a night out at the Whiskey Saloon when a man named Brett Brewer approaches him, punches him in the face, and says 'this is for Matt, he better not be convicted.' The Defendant orchestrated this assault and attempted to intimidate a witness against him. The jury should be allowed to know of this act as it is relevant and shows consciousness of guilt."

"Defense, your response?"

"Your Honor, the evidence linking my client to this assault is tenuous at best and is more prejudicial than probative. Not a scintilla of direct evidence ties my client to this assault. It very well could be that this Mr. Brewer acted totally of his own accord. The State has no proof that it the Defendant directed Mr. Brewer.

I ask that this evidence be excluded from the trial."

"I'll allow limited information that the victim has been assaulted to silence his testimony. The jury can draw their own conclusions if Mr. Brewer was acting alone or on behalf of the Defendant. Next motion, Ms. Jones you have filed a motion in limine to exclude Rachel Young's videotaped statements to the police. It's your motion. Proceed."

"Your Honor, the State intends to introduce this videotaped statement as a dying declaration, but it was not. Ms. Young had surgery from her wounds and was awake and seemed to be recovering at the point of this interview. Later, she succumbed to an infection caused by the gunshot wound and died, but for something to be a dying a declaration, the Declarant must believe that death was imminent, and she didn't. While it's true, she lapsed into a coma later that same day never to wake up again. She didn't know she was dying, and this cannot come in."

Judge Benson says, "Thank you Counsel. State your response?"

"Your Honor, this videotaped statement was actually the last words she said prior to slipping into a coma and dying and further you can hear in the video that she is still under stress from the shot, even if it isn't a dying declaration. It should come in as an excited utterance because she blurted out, 'Officer you have to arrest him. Matt shot me point blank for no reason and shot Aaron too' as soon as she saw the police officer in her room."

"Miss Jones, would you like to respond to the excited utterance argument."

I leap to my feet. "Your Honor, there is no way this can be considered an excited utterance either. This statement was made at least twenty-four hours after she was shot, after she had surgery, and after she had been in recovery. Further, it's testimonial and the Sixth Amendment guarantees my client the right to confront his accuser. I can't cross-examine a video."

"The victim's statement is out. I see no exception to the hearsay rule on that. Exchange witness and exhibit lists ten days before trial and submit jury instructions on the first day of trial."

"Matt, that went pretty well. We'll be starting trial in two weeks. You need to have clothes for court-a suit or at least a button-down shirt to look presentable."

"Mom will bring clothes to the jail. I'll tell her when she calls tonight."

"Miss Jones, are you ready to argue the Motion to Suppress on Walker?"

I change gears into the next case. "Mr. Walker was pulled over for a busted taillight. The officer ordered the driver and passenger out of the car for unknown reason while he ran their information. He wrote my client a ticket and he should have been free to leave, but then two other officers show up. The ticketing officer tells him to wait because they are going to run the K-9 officer around the vehicle. The Supreme Court held that officers cannot extend a traffic stop to use a dog absent specific reasonable suspicion to extend the stop and there was none in this case. The traffic stop was over; the dog shouldn't have been used; and the drugs found based on the dog sniff should be suppressed. Further, then the officers applied for a search warrant for my client's home based on confidential informant information and the finding of drugs in his vehicle. There is no nexus between the information and my client's home and all evidence found inside should be thrown out."

"If things are as counsel presented, I'm inclined to suppress and dismiss."

"Judge, allow me to call a witness." Judge signals for him to proceed. Coyle starts with all of the preliminary qualification questions.

"Judge for purposes of this hearing, I'll stipulate that

the officer is CLEET certified and trained in detection and investigation of drugs." I want him to get to the point.

"So stipulated. Let's get to the testimony."

"Officer, what did you pull the defendant over for?"

"His taillight was out."

"What did you do?"

"I recognized the Defendant and his passenger from prior dealings, and I was alone, so I ordered them both out of the vehicle for my safety. Then, I took the Defendant's license and the passenger's identification card and checked them for warrants. While I was doing this, another officer arrived on scene. I told him to talk to the passenger and see what was going on because they were nervous and fidgety. While Officer Hill was doing that, I finished writing the Defendant his ticket and took it to him to sign. At that point, a K-9 officer arrived on scene. Officer Hill signaled to me, and I met him back at my vehicle. At that point, Officer Hill advised me that the passenger admitted to this that there was methamphetamine in the vehicle."

"Objection the officer had no personal knowledge of what the passenger said, and his statement involves hearsay."

"Your Honor, the officer is testifying under the collective knowledge doctrine and this is for purposes of a motion hearing only, not trial."

"Allowed. There's no jury. I will take it for what it is."

"What happened then?"

"I hollered to wait for them to wait and signaled for the K-9 officer to get out and do a dog sniff. Officer Evans runs the dog around, and he alerts on the passenger side by jumping up and mounting on that side of the vehicle. Then, we begin to search the vehicle and find a large baggie of a crystal-like substance that tested positive for methamphetamine as well as a large quantity of pills that turned out to be oxycontin."

Coyle rests and the judge tells me to proceed with cross. "Officer didn't you write a report regarding this traffic stop and arrest?"

"Yes, I did," he answers.

"Are you aware that this alleged statement by the passenger is nowhere to be found in this report?"

"I thought it was. I must have forgotten to put it down."

"Isn't that a rather important piece of information to leave out of the report."

"I guess so, but she did say it and that's why I searched the vehicle."

"Isn't it also a little convenient that you remember for the first time at a motion to suppress hearing something to justify the search?"

"It's true," he admits.

Judge looks back at Coyle, "State, anything further?"

"Just argument Judge, but the officer's testimony of the passenger's statement gave him reasonable suspicion to extend the traffic stop and conduct the dog sniff. Everything from there is perfectly legit."

"Judge, the officer has never told about this statement until now. It's not trustworthy," I plead.

"Counsel, it's not my place to question the credibility of the witness. I have an officer swearing under oath that the passenger told him there was contraband in the car which justifies an extension of the traffic stop. I deny your motion."

"Judge what about the subsequent search of my client's home? The Affidavit for the warrant contains some tips that are not enough for probable cause with the additional detail that they found drugs in his car, but that doesn't justify the search of his home," I argue.

"I agree that the evidence found in the house is suppressed. This case will follow the Flowers case in the trial lineup. We are adjourned."

Coyle has his famous smirk on his face. I am fuming that that officer lied like that! I don't believe for a second that the passenger volunteered that there were drugs in the car. I will call her as a witness at trial. As I'm leaving the courtroom, I check my phone and I have some messages from Tyler with the latest vitriol that Coyle's campaign is spewing against us. "My opponent wants to put drug dealers back on the street. The only people supporting him are criminals and their bleeding-heart friends. My opponent is unqualified and soft on crime. You need a proven leader."

I text him back. "I guess he's wanting to throw the attention off our fundraiser tonight. Let's do a post emphasizing this office's penchant for locking up addicts and mentally ill and invite those who want to spend money treating people rather than locking them up to come to our fundraiser tonight."

"On it. We need to have a debate prep session with Will tomorrow night."

"I'll see if we can do it at Clara's. She will cook for us. We need to make sure we have every upcoming community event covered. Coyle is becoming even more insufferable."

"I'm most tired of reading Reid's comments about Will being unqualified when he's only been a lawyer for a couple years and wasn't in private practice long enough to know what all we deal with."

Tyler is right, but I try to limit how much time I spend reading it because my blood pressure just rises.

I feed the dogs and cats and am changing clothes into what I'm going to wear to the fundraiser when Justin walks into the bedroom. "Lindsey I'm making dinner. Want to eat with me and maybe we can talk?"

"Can't. Will has a fundraiser tonight."

"You want me to come?" He asks.

"No, I don't want to put on a show. You haven't shown up to anything so far. Why start now?"

"I'm trying Lindsey. How can I make anything right if you won't let me?"

"I don't know, Justin. I don't know. You can't rush me."

"Can we go to counseling or something?"

"We'll talk about this later." I walk past him and out to the fundraiser.

CHAPTER 17

Will and his family arrive shortly after I get there and lay out all the contributor cards and envelopes. The appetizers we have lined up look great. We have a decent turnout and unknown faces to convince them to vote for Will. Clara approaches me, "At the Salvation Army board meeting, someone was accusing Will of being an alcoholic that beats his kids. Their whisper campaign is ramping up."

"Are you having luck with the people you're talking to?"

"Overall yes, but the country club set is mostly for Coyle. We have a few allies, but they just don't want to be publicly involved."

"Michael is hosting a fundraiser for Coyle next week out there."

Will gives his speech. "I'm running for District Attorney because our community needs a change. If you think you are safer now than you were sixteen years ago, then vote to keep the status quo. If you want to feel safe in our community again, you need to elect a district attorney who will punish violent offenders: the sex offenders and child abusers harming our children, but who will also work to get treatment for those who need it. When you tag a nineteen-year-old with a felony conviction, you make it that much harder for him to get a job and be a productive citizen. When you send that addict or non-violent offender to prison, he receives a schooling on how to go on and commit more crimes. Prison doesn't help anyone. Our prisons are more overcrowded than anywhere in the world and so much of our tax dollars are paying to incarcerate people when it could be better spent on education. We need a change and I am that change."

The crowd asks some questions back and forth, and I collect some checks which helps us be able to put back to send mailers out to all the voters. Will's wife, Lucy, sits down with me at the table. "How's it going Lindsey? You seem a bit stressed."

"A bit. What about you? A couple more months to go."

"Getting really irritated with these rumors about Will. Neither I nor my children have been abused. We've ran a clean campaign and avoided negative campaigning, but to personally attack like that, is unbelievable. I've even gotten random calls saying he is having an affair. It's ridiculous."

"They are worried, or they wouldn't be going after his reputation so hard."

"What about you Lindsey? How come your husband never comes?"

"Things aren't bad right now. I found him cheating on me last week. I'm not really talking to him and he's living in the guest bedroom."

"I'm so sorry. Do you need anything?"

"No. Just trying to deal with it. This gives me an excuse to be out of the house for an evening and I am glad for that."

"We better take some good pictures. Go get with Will and we'll get some family shots."

Lucy signals for her daughters and Will to come over and I take some pictures. I also take a picture of Tyler and Will and various pictures of Will with people there. These will look great on the website.

As the guests file out, "Tomorrow at 6, I'll have dinner as

we prepare for the debate."

"That's good enough reason to come."

"For sure, I think she should cook every time we have a meeting." I smile at her.

"That's unanimous. I'll probably have Lily with me tomorrow."

"You know we love her." Will and Tyler both have great kids, but Lily is a political operative in the making.

"I spoke to Lions club today and had a good reception. I stayed talking to people for about two hours. I've been going to the Masons. Coyle isn't attending any of these groups from what I can tell."

"Good to hear. Keep it up. It looks like Coyle and I are gearing up to go head to head in a murder trial in a couple weeks. Hopefully, I get a not guilty and that gives him some bad press as well."

"Did you see he was on the news last night for filing for the death penalty on a child murder? After I've been talking about that for six months?"

"No, I missed that, but I'm not surprised.."

"He's also posting about starting diversion courts which has also been on our materials since the beginning."

"He has no original thoughts or ideas."

We all say our goodbyes and head home. I get home around 8:00 P.M. and Justin is sitting in the living room and I notice that there is a new couch and the one their transgression took place on has been removed.

"You got rid of the couch?"

"I knew you wouldn't ever sit on it again, so I bought a new one and sold this one to a lady I work with." He gives me a weak smile.

I am genuinely relieved that the couch is gone. I must admit that was thoughtful of him. I walk on past into the bedroom and get into pajamas, but I go back into the living room, but it is the first time I've really sat with him since this all happened. He looks at me and smiles. We sit in an awkward silence, but it gets a little easier as the night wears on. It's ten o'clock, so I head to bed.

CHAPTER 18

Trial starts Monday! Time to clear my desk of everything I have pending so I can totally focus on Matt's case. I continue any cases that I have set in other counties and file several miscellaneous motions in my domestic and civil cases.

I make an outline of everything I want to cover in voir dire or jury selection. It's one thing you don't really practice in mock trial, and it's a part not covered on television or movies. It's the one time you directly talk to a judge. For this one, I want to get jurors that are gun owners. People that have had some experience with people on drugs. Drugs cut both ways in this case. My client was using drugs, but one of the victims was a drug dealer. I want to talk about lying and judging credibility. The usual things about the standard of beyond a reasonable doubt.

I type, erase, and retype parts of an opening statement. I prepare my trial files and label all my exhibits and print out my sheets for each witness. I feel about as prepared as I can for the trial. I've done several trials with Coyle, and I can almost guess what he is going to say so I tweak my defense to combat it.

I go ahead and get my second trial file ready since I will be doing back to back trials. The second trial will be easier than the first because it's officers only and no victims. After these trials are over, I need to get to the task of hiring a new assistant too. I've had to do my own filing lately and that's extra hours I could put towards cases.

I have a counseling appointment this afternoon, but I

didn't invite Justin. I first wanted to see if I liked her first and see what I really think before we went to any counseling together. I'm waiting in the lobby when a lady in her forties with red hair comes out and calls, "Lindsey?" I stand up follow her around the corner to her office and sit on a couch—very typical counselor's office with a couch. I'm already not sure how I feel about this.

"Lindsey, I'm Aria James. It's nice to meet you. Tell me a little about yourself and why you're here"

"I'm Lindsey. I'm an attorney. I'm married to my high school sweetheart who I found having sex with my assistant a couple weeks ago. He's living in our guest bedroom. We're barely speaking. I can barely stand to look at him. He's tried to apologize, and he's wanted to talk, but I just haven't been able to do it."

"Were you shocked by this affair?"

"Stunned. I never thought he would cheat on me."

"How was your marriage prior to that?"

"We had drifted apart but about normal I guess."

"When you think of your life five years from now, what do you see?"

I think for a minute. "I don't know. I want my firm to continue to expand. Maybe have a full-time assistant and employ an investigator on a more regular basis. Maybe have an intern or another associate."

"And at home? Is Justin there? Are you alone? Is someone else there?"

"I don't know. I can't make it out. I can't imagine Justin not being in my life. He knows me better than anyone. He's my best friend, but it's like he's not him anymore. I hate being at home. I avoid him." I know this sounds stupid.

"You're wounded. The issue is whether you think you can move past it and if you two can build a better relationship. It will be hard and take some work, but is that what you want, or do you want to start over alone?"

"I still don't know what happened. I looked up phone records and they had been talking for about six weeks and it ended when I found them, but who knows how it would have gone on if I hadn't? I work all the time and he doesn't want to focus on work. We don't have fun together like we used to. I knew that, but I just didn't expect this.."

"It's not your fault Lindsey. Marriage requires constant work by both parties, but that doesn't give any an excuse to cheat."

"I know but I've been unhappy with the state of our marriage anyway. Are we just together because it's comfortable or because we really love each other and should be together? Love doesn't conquer all or last."

"Why don't you try having a conversation with Justin? It's going to be a new experience because you haven't talked now for a while. Just talk and see how you feel and then why don't you two come to counseling and we can try to work on these issues. We can explore if the cheating is the problem or if the relationship is the problem and whether or not you can overcome."

I like her. I feel like I can talk to her. I'll consider doing counseling with Justin with her and just some on my own as well, but I also need to really think about what I want. *Do I want to be married and have a family or do I want my career, or do I want both? Am I too involved with my clients? Am I too obsessed with the fight and using that to not live my own life? Is there more to life than work? What do I want my life to be like? I am a workaholic, and I realize that in a way that is selfish because it's about achieving success and honor. Is my entire identity wrapped up in being a lawyer? What is essence of me?*

I go home and change into jeans and think about what Aria said and play through possible conversations in my head with Justin. I've known him since I was ten. We've been in a relationship since we were fourteen and I'm rehearsing how to talk to him. How has my life come to this? I decide to cook dinner-a simple Mexican casserole of chicken, queso, cheeses, and tortilla chips. I also decide I want some brownies. I'm going to eat my emotions.

Justin comes in as I'm pulling the food out of the oven. "That smells good."

"I'm about to serve it. You can eat with me if you want." It's a struggle to get the words out.

"That would be great! I'll make us some drinks and get the silverware." He has a grin on his face and looks like a teenager again. I make two plates and take them to the dining room and sit down across from him. I still can't really look at him, but at least we are sitting together.

"How's work?"

"My murder trial starts on Monday and then I have a drug trafficking case to follow that."

A few minutes of awkward silence follow as we eat until Justin breaks in, "This shouldn't be so hard Lindsey. We've been together for twenty years."

"And your cheating on me broke that bond," I snap.

"I know Lindsey, and I'm so sorry. There's no excuse, but I already felt like I lost you. We stopped being us. I miss us."

"I know. Maybe we've grown too far apart."

"I'm not ready to give up on us."

"I'm willing to try counseling, but no promises. I saw one

today. I think she might be able to help us if we can be helped.

"Justin, how did it happen with Emily? I really want to know."

"She came by the house to bring the truck back after she used it to run errands for you. She came to the door and knocked. I had a meeting out of the office that afternoon, so I came home early. I let her in, and she gave me the keys and left me your files. I didn't have a t-shirt on, and she rubbed my arm and made a comment that she could tell I worked out and didn't look like an accountant. She was wearing a low-cut top and short skirt and it just went from there." He can't make eye contact with me.

"How many times did it happen?"

"Three and the time that you walked in. We met two other times at hotels. She was sexting me and we flirted back and forth, but it was just physical. There was nothing emotional about it. I didn't care about her. It was just something exciting and different. It was thoughtless Lins, and I'm sorry."

I nod. "Don't you think I've had offers? I would like attention from someone else too, but I never gave anyone an opening. I'm loyal. How can I ever trust you again?" I get up from the table then and go into my bedroom. I need to escape from my reality.

CHAPTER 19

I book a massage and a manicure and pedicure to help me relax on this Saturday before this trial. I love the feeling of a massage because you can't do anything but lay there. The lights are dim and soothing music plays. My neck and shoulders are so full of knots and stay super tense. My mind is emptied of thoughts and worries and while this massage is happening. I also booked things to keep me away from the house to avoid Justin.

I am at the nail salon sitting with my feet in the hot soapy water as Regan joins me in the seat next to me. "Hey Regan, glad you were able to make it."

"Yes, me too. I'm long overdue and we both have a terribly busy week this next week with the murder trial." She starts soaking her feet.

"What color did you pick today?"

She shows me a dark lavender. "What about you?"

I show her a very traditional red. "Going with tradition for the trial."

"How are you holding up Lins?"

"We talked a little bit last night, but it ended with me practically bolting back into the bedroom. After the trial, we are going to try couple's counseling. I just don't know Regan. He did replace the couch for me."

"That's good about the couch, but seriously I'm glad you

tried to talk, but I'm sorry it's so painful."

"How's Chris?"

"Something is wrong with him. He's just so irritable and short-tempered. I just can't reach him. We aren't connecting anymore. I wish he would go to counseling with me, but I'm afraid he'll just get mad if I suggest it."

"It can't hurt to try."

"That's true. You want to grab a bite after this?"

I open my book to read. As weird as it sounds, I'm a lawyer that enjoys reading legal thrillers. I'm reading the latest John Grisham novel. If I'm not reading a legal thriller, then it is usually romance novels by Danielle Steele or Sandra Brown: always something that doesn't require a lot of thought and is for enjoyment. About an hour later, we went to eat at our local Chili's and stuffed ourselves and we went our separate ways.

REGAN

I walk into my house and it smells fresh and clean, so I look around and notice that the carper has been shampooed. "Watch your step. The carpet is still wet, and I just mopped."

"What got into you?"

"I know you've been working really hard and you will be busy next week with that trial so I thought it would be good for you to not have to worry about cleaning the house. Your nails look nice."

"Thanks, Hun. What do you want to do today?"

"Why don't you look and see what movies are playing? We haven't done that in a while. I thought that we could go see one and then go out and eat a nice dinner out and then we can have some fun when we get back. We haven't had one of our nights in a while."

This is the man I married: the one that is my best friend. "Well are you in the mood for action or thriller or a comedy?"

"I don't care babe. You pick. I'm going to take a shower and go get ready," he answers and gives her a kiss on the top of the head. Suddenly, she's glad she got her nails done, so she picks out a nice outfit and touches up her hair and make-up.

Chris pulls out a couple shirts and shoes and jeans and asks which outfit I like best. He's a guy who cares about his clothes and that they match. He is rather picky. I pick the gray shirt with the Calvin Klein jeans and the airwalks. "You look nice, babe."

I picked a thriller to make him happy and give me an excuse to lean into him. We sat in the back-holding hands.

Afterwards we went out for a nice steak and the waitress flirts with him as always happens. He can't help but turn on the charm. "Chris, that waitress is completely ignoring me. She hasn't refilled my drink once but yours is never low. 'Do you need anything else sir?' Waitress is actually actively ignoring me."

"Do you want me to show her my wedding ring? Or maybe I should just take her to the bathroom and bang her out?"

"Stop it. You're ridiculous, but you don't have to be so charming all the time."

We leave the restaurant and just drive around in the car enjoying the quiet and listening to music. It's something we do. "It's nice. Let's sit out on the back porch for a while. We can bring the telescope out."

"That sounds nice."

He sets up the telescope and I gaze for a while. We both take turns looking at the clear blue sky. We think that we spot some drones. Then, we settle in and talk about anything and everything. Before long, it's after midnight and they head inside.

SHELLEY L. LEVISAY

I put on a silk nightgown and robe and slide into bed and he crawls in with just his boxers on and he kisses me. A real kiss: one we haven't shared quite a while, and both fall asleep in each other's arms.

CHAPTER 20

It's finally the day of Matt's trial. I put on a very conservative black skirt suit with white button-down blouse and medium size heels. I arrive at the courthouse at 8:30 for the final call docket before the trials start. They managed to bring Matt in his trial clothes, and he looks decent. The jurors are still checking in and they are filling out their jury questionnaires and the district judge will give them instructions. It will be another couple of hours before we start picking a jury.

Voir Dire is the French phrase for "to speak the truth." That is the proper name for jury selection. It is one area of a trial that is not covered by television or movies or in mock trial competitions, but it is incredibly important. It's the one time you as an attorney get to interact directly with a jury. It's when you first get them to start to like you. It's more of jury deselection because you must decide who will hurt your case or be too biased against your client. In this case, I want to get rid of people that are anti-guns and hate illegal drugs or have been a victim of violent crime.

Judge Benson starts with his usual speech, "You are all eligible to serve as jurors, but you may not be the right jurors for this case. I and the attorneys are going to ask you some questions that are designed to pick the fairest jurors to both Mr. Flowers and to the State. None of the questions are meant to embarrass or bring up painful memories but to determine if there are any biases that would interfere with this case. If there is any question you don't feel comfortable with answering in front of everyone, just let me know and you can approach the bench and answer those questions."

He then begins with some introductory questions about if any of them have served as jurors before. He also asks if any of them have ever been on trial in a civil or criminal case. He follows up by asking if any of them have ever testified as a witness in court before. A few of them answer each question, but none of the answers are unusual. "How many of you have ever been a victim of a crime?"

Several hands shoot up at that point. Benson starts at the end of the back row. Several have been victims of burglaries-either having their homes or cars broken into and most the crimes were never solved., "I was robbed at gunpoint while working as a clerk at a gas station."

"That's sound like a terrible experience. How long ago was that?"

\"It was about five years ago."

"What happened to the person who robbed you?"

"He was arrested about a week later and he went to prison."

"Did you have to testify?"

"No, it didn't go to trial. I guess he pled to it."

"Is there anything about that experience that you think would color your ability to judge this case fairly and on its own merits?"

"No, I can be fair in this case." Everyone says that unless they are trying to get kicked off the jury. Who wants to admit that they are going to be biased and unfair? I put a star here to do some follow up to see if she is pro-prosecution.

Another man says, "My son was shot in a drive-by shooting." This isn't good I think to myself. He is going to have a bias against gun crimes even if it is subconsciously.

"I'm sorry to hear that. Was that here and when was that?"

"About fifteen years ago in Chicago. It was a drug deal gone wrong. He was just in the wrong place at the wrong time.." This just gets worse with this guy. I put an x in his box. None of the other answers cause me any real alarm.

He asks about family members or close friends in law enforcement. Several them have some connection to a police officer, but nothing out of the ordinary. In this case, my defense doesn't depend on not believing the officers. It will come down to if they believe the victim or my client or neither.

Judge then finishes his set of questions. "Now the attorney for the State will ask you questions."

Coyle, as the State, goes first. We have done a few trials together and I can almost perform his voir dire selection. He always asks a lot of questions about people and their kids. People always like talking about their kids, and he uses that to talk about credibility of witnesses. He also uses an example of circumstantial evidence that involves a child being accused of stealing a plate of cookies and a parent finding the child with chocolate on his face. Another one that people sometimes use is going to bed and waking up to a white substance on the ground: you can infer that it snowed even though you did not see the snow.

Coyle veers off his usual script by asking, "There are no swans in the sewer. How many of you have ever heard that expression?" Several people raise their hands. I see where he is going with this. His star witness is a drug dealer and he knows it. The victim was either an accomplice to her boyfriend's drug dealing or at a minimum a drug addict.

"You may hear some testimony about the victim or witnesses in this case being involved in drugs, do you think that makes it ok for that person to be a victim?" Of course, everyone says no or shakes their head.

"Have any of you had any family members or close friends that struggled with addiction?" Several hands shoot up. This line of questioning tells me some things that I need to know so this is helpful. "Ms. Owens who in your life dealt with that issue?"

"My nephew got hooked on meth and lost his job and his kids and eventually went to jail."

"Would you want a jury to treat your nephew with fairness if he became a victim even though he made some bad decisions?"

"Of course, that doesn't mean he deserves to be a victim, but his using drugs might put him in a bad environment." She could be helpful to me.

He poses a general question to the panel, "What do you think about legalization of drugs?" No one speaks for a minute. "Now I know some of you have opinions?"

One man speaks up. "I don't think they should be illegal. The government should stay out of it. If someone wants to ruin their life, then so be it."

Another woman argues, "I think people using drugs need to be punished because it doesn't just ruin their life, it affects their families and usually they commit other crimes too."

Yet another woman says, "To me it would depend what drug you are talking about. Not all of them are that dangerous, and some of the prescribed medications are just as dangerous and people abuse those and alcohol too."

Those statements are decent cross-section of the community and their views on drugs. I write down who said what.

Next, he goes into a line of questioning about having

to prove elements of a crime and using a BLT sandwich as a comparison. A BLT has bacon, lettuce, tomato, and bread to be a sandwich. He says that the type of bacon or tomato is only a detail and not an element.

I don't care for Coyle, but he is a good trial lawyer mostly because he does relate well with juries. His voir dire takes forever. About two hours in, Judge Benson declares, "Jury we will break for lunch now. Return at 1:30 and report to the jury room and my bailiff will bring you into the courtroom." We all stand for the jury as they exit.

Judge Benson asks as he will on all breaks if we have anything for the record outside the presence of the jury.

The jailer takes my client back to the jail to have his lunch. If he stays at the courthouse, he will not get to eat. That has been a battle we have fought before, but the jailers will not allow them to eat any outside food.

I walk directly to Regan. "Want to go grab lunch nearby?" I always take shorter lunches during trial because I will go over my voir dire and opening statement before we go back on the record.

Honestly, at this point with the questions that have already been asked, I have a good idea of who my preemptory challenges will be. I know the State still probably has another hour or more to go on this issue. Thankfully, this case did not have too much media attention or that would be another issue that would delay things. Both sides get to strike five jurors for whatever reason. While jury selection is to pick your jury and an alternate, if done correctly, it is also a great way to weave your theory of the case in early, so the jurors are already thinking about the issues before they hear the witnesses and see the evidence.

Regan and I go to the sandwich shop downtown nearby and settle down to eat. I "How was the rest of your weekend?"

"Amazing. Chris and I had a great night out and the rest of Saturday night and lazed around on Sunday. He was my husband again."

"That's great. Glad you had a good weekend. What do you think about the jury so far?" I ask her.

"About as good as any we normally have, I suppose, but Coyle needs to wrap it up. I'm tired of hearing his voice."

"I know right? I thought it was just me."

"How are things going with Justin?"

"Kind of on hold for the moment. I told him I needed to focus on this trial. We are going to start counseling afterwards."

We finish our lunches and head back. I go back to my office for about thirty minutes and practice my opening lines for the jury.

Coyle goes back to the podium and starts in on part of his voir dire that I fundamentally disagree with. "We as the State have the burden of proof and have to prove our case beyond a reasonable doubt. We only have to prove those elements of the BLT. I can't define it for you, and neither can the defense, but it does not mean beyond all doubt or beyond a shadow of a doubt. That means you can still have a doubt that is reasonable. It is not your job to look for doubt. Can you promise to only hold me to my burden and not to anything more?" The jurors nod their heads. He calls out a few jurors specifically to ask them if they will only hold them to that burden and not more. Then he passes the panel for cause.

I step up to the podium with the notes I took during Coyle's turn and also took my outline of questions I wanted to cover. "Ladies and gentlemen, as Judge Benson told you, I'm Lindsey Jones, Matthew Flower's attorney. I promise I will not take as much times as my predecessor because he has covered some of the important areas already. I want to start by asking, 'How many of you when you walked in and saw my client thought he was innocent?'"

When no one raises their hand, "Why not? We have the presumption of innocence in this country. He is presumed to be innocent unless and until the State proves beyond a reasonable doubt that he committed murder and assault and battery with a deadly weapon. At this point, you have heard nothing but the charges. You understand that he is innocent?" Finally, some heads start nodding.

"Even so, how many of you think 'Well he had to do something, or he wouldn't be here?'" A couple of people raise their hands, I address the first one, "Mrs. Powell, why do you say that?"

"I don't think the police and the district attorney charge people for no reason."

"We certainly hope they wouldn't do that on purpose, don't we?" I suggest and she nods. "Have you heard any news stories about wrongfully convicted inmates being released from prison?"

"Yes I have. I would hope that's rare."

"Yes, we would hope that, but you understand sometimes the police get it wrong. Sometimes the district attorney gets it wrong and that's why we start with everyone being innocent." I talk to her but make eye contact with the rest of the jury.

I look at the other man. "Mr. Watson, what do you think about the famous old saying 'It is better for ten guilty men to go free than for one innocent man to suffer.'"

"I don't want to convict someone who is innocent, but I don't like the idea of guilty people getting away with crime either."

"Fair enough sir, but as Mr. Flowers sits here right now what would your verdict be?"

"It would have to be not guilty because I haven't heard any evidence."

"Yes, that's correct, now do you all agree that Mr. Flowers is not guilty at this time and you will vote for a verdict of not guilty unless the States proves their case beyond a reasonable doubt?" I go down the line on this one.

"Now Mr. Coyle talked to you about elements, now do each of you promise to hold the State to proving all of those elements even in these serious charges as murder and assault and battery with a deadly weapon. Would any of you have a hard time returning a verdict of not guilty on such serious charges?" I look throughout the panel.

"How many of you own a gun?" Thankfully, almost two-thirds of the panel raises their hand.

"How many of you have your conceal carry permit?" About half of them raise their hand.

"Have any of you ever had to defend yourself with that gun?" A couple of people raise their hand. The first is an older man, I turn to him, "Mr. White, can you tell us about that?"

"I served in Vietnam and I had to kill some people,"."

"Mr. White, in your service, what were you trained to do or think if someone pointed a gun at you?"

"That they mean to kill you,"."

"What would you do if someone pointed a gun at you?"

"I would kill him before he could kill me. Shoot first and ask questions later. Better him than me." This earns a few chuckles.

"So, if someone points a gun at you, you would take that as an attack against you then?" He nods, then I pose to the panel. "Anyone disagree with that?" Everyone nods their heads.

"Mrs. Johnson, I saw you raised your hands that you had to use a gun to defend yourself, tell us about that?"

"A guy broke into my house. I heard the window shatter and I ran back to my bedroom and grabbed my shotgun. When I heard the man approaching, I clicked my shotgun and when he heard that, he ran away. I called police and they caught him a few blocks away."

"That's quite a story. Did you have any hesitation to use that gun had that man continued advancing toward you?"

"Not at all. My daddy taught me to shoot when I was young and I'm not going to go down without a fight." Several other jurors murmur agreement. This jury panel is looking up.

"Last question, and I'm going to ask each one of you. If you were in Mr. Flower's position facing life in prison, are you the type of juror you would want to decide your fate?" I ask and go down the line and they all answer yes. After that I passed the panel for cause.

"Counsel, gather your notes and decide your preemptory challenges and approach the bench." I lean over and confer with Matt and show him my notes of who I want to strike.

"I trust you, and I really didn't like these two." He points to a couple on my list.

"Ok Matt, we're about to get your jury."

We alternate with our strikes and then the Judge excuses those we struck, and we have our jury. I document the names and positions in the box of each juror. Now we must do it all again with an alternate but it's much abbreviated version and we get our alternate quickly.

Judge Benson says, "Counsel approach." We both walk to the bench and he states, "it's already pretty late in the day and I think the jury has had enough, why don't we start with opening statements tomorrow? Any objection?"

Both of us agree with him. "Ladies and gentlemen, we will always try to end the day by 5 P.M. and so we don't run late, we are going to adjourn for the day after I give you your oath. Return tomorrow by 9 A.M. in the jury room and the bailiff will bring you down. Now all of you rise and answer, "Each of you have been selected as jurors, do each of you agree to truly listen to the evidence and try this case and follow all instructions I give you?" They all answer, "I do."

"With that you are dismissed until tomorrow." We all rise again as the jury exits. I gather all of my notes and file together to leave and tell Matt, "We will start with opening statements and witnesses tomorrow. I feel good about our jury. Get a good night's sleep and remember to stay neutral and calm regardless of what is said tomorrow."

"Yes ma'am, I will do my best. Thank you so much for all you are doing."

Glenda has been sitting in all day during the jury selection process and approaches me as I leave. "How do you think it's going Lindsey?"

"It's going as well as it can right now. I think I made some headway with the jury and we got as good of a panel as we could. Go home and get some rest. The judge will sequester all witnesses tomorrow so you probably will not be able to sit in and listen to the other witnesses."

"Why not? I want to be there for my son."

"Because if you hear the other witnesses then you could change your testimony to help your son. The State's witnesses cannot sit in either. This is for the best. You might just get upset anyway. I'll keep you as updated as I can. Matt will know you're here and that you support him."

I have a headache as I often do at the end of a day of trial because I must be hyper-focused on everything. I head home, change into comfortable clothes, and sit down in my chair to relax for a minute. Justin comes in. "I was going to make some hamburgers, is that ok with you?"

"That's fine I probably won't eat much. I'll be reviewing all of my notes again and then trying to relax."

"How did the first day go?" He asks.

"We picked our jury. We didn't get further. So far so good. You know it's too early to tell."

"Good luck. I'll bring you some food when it's ready and leave you to it."

"Thanks, I appreciate that." with that I silently practice my opening to myself and then pace and say it aloud a few times. I barely touch my dinner when he brings it. When I feel satisfied, I have my opening down pat, I go take a nice long hot bubble bath and go to bed early.

CHAPTER 21

Day two of trial is here and we get into the meat of the trial. The State goes first of course because they have the burden of proof. It looks bleak when the State is presenting their case. You walk a fine line between making all your defense points and objecting, while also not irritating the jury or looking like you are hiding anything.

When I walk into the courtroom, my client is already present with the jailer and thankfully they let him wear a different shirt from yesterday. It's always best to have different clothes for your clients so it isn't obvious to the jury that they are in jail because jurors cannot help but be prejudiced by that: also, why defendants are not cuffed in front of the jury. Most jailers try not to make it obvious, but sometimes the jury figures it out anyway.

First Assistant Coyle comes in with all his files and evidence and lays them out on his table. He has another assistant district attorney helping him, but he is handling all the trial work. It is nice to have a second chair to bounce ideas off, to help you make sure you get everything in that you want, and logistically to help things run smoothly.

After the jury sits down, Coyle stands up and addresses the jury first by reading through the Information and I tune out. Then, he pauses and gets to the point, "Ladies and gentlemen of the jury, Mr. Flowers shot and killed Rachel Graves in cold blood, after first shooting her boyfriend Aaron West in the shoulder. The evidence will show that the Defendant was going to rob Mr. West and Ms. Graves and when they wouldn't comply, he shot them. The evidence will show that the Defendant would stop at nothing to feed his methamphetamine habit. You will hear how Rachel at first survived her painful injuries after surgery but succumbed to an infection while in the hospital and never left. Aaron will tell you how the gunshot to his shoulder tore threw him and he struggles with pain still to this day. This crime didn't have to happen. Aaron didn't have to get shot. Rachel didn't have to die, but this Defendant cared more about his drugs than about human life. Value the life of Rachel Graves and protect Aaron West and the rest of society from this Defendant by finding him guilty and sending him to prison for the rest of his life."

I could have objected to that last statement, but I knew he was ending and sometimes it turns off juries to interrupt the other lawyer. The judge looks at me and asks, "Ms. Jones do you want to give your opening now or reserve it?"

"Now, Your Honor," I answer and stand and move toward the podium. I could waive and wait until the start of my case, but I don't like to leave the jury with nothing from me after they hear the State's opening. I want my opening ringing in their ears as the State starts its case.

"Three people with guns. Three people on methamphetamine. Three people were shot. Ladies and gentlemen, this case is not as cut and dry as the State makes it out to be. The evidence will show that three people know what happened that night. The deceased, Mr. West, and Mr. Flowers. The evidence will show that Mr. West is patently unreliable, has a long rap sheet, and is an active drug dealer. The evidence will show that my client is young man who caught up in a situation and had to make a split-second decision to save his life. My client acted in self-defense and only fired to save his own life. At the end of this trial, ladies and gentlemen, I believe you will find that he was justified in his actions and you will return a not guilty verdict. I ask you to do just that. Thank you."

As soon as I sit down, Judge Benson says, "State call your

first witness."

Coyle stands and bellows, "The State calls Christy Shannon." A short woman with brown hair walks in. I know from the evidence that she is the 911 dispatcher who took the first call. The judge swears her in and tells Coyle to proceed.

"Ma'am what do you do for a living?"

"I'm a dispatcher for the county. I am the supervisor of the department."

"What is your job description?"

"I answer 911 calls and attempt to help the callers. I get the information that I can about what is going on and where so I can dispatch police, ambulances, or fire depending on the situation and sometimes all three."

He asks the qualifying questions and offers the 911 call as Exhibit 1. I don't object because there is no point, and it would come in anyway. The Judge grants him permission to play it.

"911 what's the address to your emergency?"

"My girlfriend's been shot! I've been shot. Send an ambulance right now!" The caller screams talking at a mile a minute.

"Ok sir, what's the address to your emergency?"

"She's bleeding out I've got to have help now." The caller continues without allowing the dispatcher to even finish.

"Sir I need you to calm down and answer my questions. Where are you?"

"We're off highway 3. 39058 E. 1st Street," he says and then adds quickly, "Come quickly. I've got to try to help my girlfriend." The caller then hangs up.

He finishes and there's no reason to cross her.

"Call your next, Mr. Coyle," Judge Benson directs.

"The State calls Henry Butler," Coyle says.

The man walks in wearing his paramedic uniform. This is important for the State to establish injuries, but I may be able to get a few things for me out of this witness as well.

Coyle starts his questioning with the usual, "How are you employed sir?"

"I am a paramedic."

"How long have you been in that line of work?"

"This is my thirteenth year."

"On May 17th last year did you respond to a shooting?"

"Yes, I did. I responded out to old highway 3 for what I thought was going to be two shooting victims, but it turned out there were three victims."

"Would you describe the scene?"

"It was trailer home in the country big property. When we pulled in, we saw the Defendant lying face down in the grass. My partner started to check him out and I walked toward the house where I saw a man waving his arms and screaming, 'In here, help us!'"

"What did you do then?"

"I went in to help the woman with the gunshot wound to the stomach. There was blood everywhere and I attempted to stop the bleeding and bandage as well as I could. There were other police and paramedics there by that time, so we get her on a gurney to transport her to the nearest hospital. She needed immediate surgery."

"Can you describe Ms. Graves's injuries?"

"She had a serious gun show wound to her center

abdomen. A few centimeters to the left and the wound would have hit her aorta and she would have already been dead."

"What about Mr. West what were his injuries?"

"His injuries were not severe though I did bandage him, and he went to the hospital for stitches. He was shot in the upper arm and came out through his shoulder."

Coyle finishes and I start my cross. "Mr. Butler, what kind of injuries did my client Mr. Flowers have?"

"My partner really treated him, but I saw him briefly and was the supervisor on scene that processed all of the records. He was shot in the back of the leg."

"What part of the leg if you know?"

"I believe it was the back of the thigh."

"Was Mr. Flowers also transported to the hospital and treated?"

"Yes, I believe he needed surgery to repair the wound. It did some damage internally. The wound was close to the femoral artery."

"Did Mr. West have to have surgery?"

"I don't believe so. His would was relatively minor compared to the other two gunshot wounds."

We take our morning break then. During the break I went downstairs to the vending machine trying to avoid jurors to get a Dr. Pepper. I see I have about ten messages from Lea, so I scan through them, but I don't have enough time to respond to them. I see that one of the messages is that a potential client has already called twice and it's not even noon. I think to myself; I don't think I want to deal with this client if they are already this needy or I'm going to quote a huge retainer. I go back into chambers to visit with the bailiff Sherrie. We show each other our latest pictures of our dogs. Then it's time to go back.

Judge Benson says, "Mr. Coyle call your next witness."

"The State calls Jacob Wilson." The deputy comes in and the Judge swears him in. "Would you please state your name and occupation for the record?"

"Jacob Wilson, and I'm a deputy with the Sheriff's Office."

"How long have you been in law enforcement?"

"For two years at the Sheriff's office."

"Were you the first officer on a scene on Old Highway 3 on May 17th of last year?"

"Yes, I was the first officer, but ambulance and fire were already there. They pulled in just ahead of me."

"Can you describe the scene when you arrived?"

"It was dark about 11:30 P.M. when I got there. The property was a couple acres off a dirt road. It was an isolated property with a large trailer back behind a long driveway that was about the size of a football field. The Defendant was lying face down in the grass close to the road. I saw a gun near him."

Coyle interrupts, "Let me stop you there. You said you saw the Defendant, for the record can you identify who you are talking about?"

"Matthew Flowers he is sitting at the left table next to his attorney."

"And did he have a gun?"

"Yes, he had a Glock .9mm a few feet from him that he could easily have grabbed. So, I secured that gun and handcuffed him for officer safety. The paramedic began treating him at that time."

"Did the Defendant say anything to you?" I'm about to

stand and object because I haven't been provided with any statements for anything at this time, but the witness answered, "All he said was 'help me.' He appeared to be in pain."

"What did you see and do next?"

"I made my way up to the driveway and talked to Mr. West who had blood all down the front of his shirt. He's talking very quickly saying 'he shot me and my girlfriend. You've got to help her.' Then, I went inside, and the paramedics were working on Rachel. She was in and out of consciousness at that time. While I'm looking around the room, I see several more guns and I started securing them. I also noticed some used syringes and pipes that I know through my training and experience to be methamphetamine pipes. I called the on-call detective Investigator Goins to tell him what was going on."

"What kinds of guns did you see?"

"A .45, a Deringer, a shotgun, and a .380 revolver."

"You stated you saw drug paraphernalia did you see any drugs?"

"Yes, I saw a baggie with what looked like methamphetamine."

"Judge, may I approach?"

"You may."

"Deputy, I'm going to show you some pictures, tell me if these pictures accurately represent the scene you arrived on?" Coyle questions as he walks to the witness.

Deputy Wilson looks through the stack of pictures. "Yes this is what the scene looked like."

"Did you take these pictures?"

"Yes, I took these. Investigator Goins took more later."

"Your Honor, I offer State's Exhibits 3-10."

"Ms. Jones?"

"Your Honor, may I approach and see what he's offering?" I ask.

"Yes of course, Mr. Coyle in the future show exhibits to opposing counsel first." Coyle nods. I move forward and they are all pictures I have been given in discovery and I want to use some of these myself.

"No objection, Your Honor." I move back to my seat.

"What did you do next?"

"I tried to preserve the scene by setting up the evidence tape and putting markers down where I saw any evidence."

"No further questions."

"Ms. Jones, cross?"

"Yes, Your Honor." I say and take some of my own pictures and notes with me to the lectern. "Deputy Wilson, I'm showing you a diagram that was prepared by the Sheriff's office, did you prepare this?"

"No, Investigator Goins did that."

"Is this an accurate diagram of the scene though?"

"It appears to be yes."

"I would offer this as Defense Exhibit 1." I'm playing a strategy game, I want to make some small points, but not tip my whole hand to the prosecution.

Coyle can't object or he would stupid to a jury to object to a diagram made by law enforcement.

"Deputy, I'm putting a copy of that same diagram up for the jury to see, can you tell the jury what the circles represent?"

"The circles are where blood was found."

"So, there was blood both inside and outside the trailer correct?"

"Yes, a lot inside and some a few feet from the door and then close to where we found the Defendant."

"There seems to be a lot of blood inside the house both in the main room where Ms. Graves was shot and goes into a bedroom off that room and then circles back. Can you explain that?"

"The blood trail seemed to go towards a safe into the bedroom back out to the living room."

"What about the 'x's?"

"Those are .45 shell casings."

"Now, you spoke to Mr. West at the scene, didn't you?"

"Yes, I did to get his version of what happened?"

"Did you make any determinations about his level of impairment?"

"I didn't perform any specific tests or anything like that."

I'm sure he doesn't want to come out and say it because it hurts their version, so I continue, "You saw evidence of drug use in the home correct?"

"Yes."

"You mentioned you found drug paraphernalia, what kind?"

"Needles, baggies, pipes, scales."

"What in your training and experience are scales used for?"

"For measuring and weighing drugs for sale."

"Did you make a determination about the amount of drugs and paraphernalia?"

"I thought there was possible use and dealing of drugs, which I advised the detective."

"Did Mr. West appear to be high that night?"

"It's quite possible that he was, but like I said, that wasn't really what I was focused on,."

"You're trained to recognize levels of intoxication, aren't you?"

"Yes, I am."

"And in your training and experience what impression did you form about his intoxication level?"

"It appeared that he was under the influence of a stimulant."

"And methamphetamine is a stimulant, correct?"

"Yes." I finish and Judge Benson then adjourns us for lunch.

CHAPTER 22

I met Nick at a cafe near the courthouse for lunch and to recap the trial thus far. He's already seated when I arrive, so I sit down across from him. "Hey, how's the trial going thus far?"

"As well as it can so far, I think anyway. I've made the points about all of them being shot. I subtly let them know that Aaron chased my client shooting at him. It's all going to come down to whether they believe Matt."

"Or they could not believe any of them and hopefully find reasonable doubt."

"Yes, I always hammer reasonable doubt and hope they are listening, but you know jurors don't like to let people off on serious crimes even if they are innocent."

"Lins, are you ok? You've seemed stressed more than usual lately."

"Yes and no. I walked in on Justin cheating on me with my assistant. We're currently living in different bedrooms at the house. After this is over, we are going to try counseling."

"Do you really want to make it work? How happy were you to begin with?" He quips—always getting right to the point.

"I don't know. I love Justin, but we have grown apart. We aren't the same people we were at fifteen when we were first together: both of us have let things go. He's the only guy I've ever been with romantically, so, of course, sometimes I wonder if I would be happier with someone else, but at the same time, I took a vow for better or worse. It's destroyed a piece in me that he violated those vows. I can barely talk to him."

"If you aren't going to be happy, you might want to end it now. Infidelity is usually a symptom that something else is wrong. Were y'all happy in bed? Sorry, is that too personal?"

"It is pretty personal. Like I said we've been together seventeen years, but we didn't have sex together until we were married, but we've been married twelve years. I think it's normal for people that have been married this long, but we still have sex regularly. We aren't in the honeymoon phase anymore and lovey dovey all the time, but not horrible."

"Men get bored. It really may not have meant anything to him, you know."

"I know that. It doesn't make it hurt any less, but I admit it. He didn't think I was paying attention to him. I may have been interested in my work than in him lately. What's sad is after he had the affair, he started trying harder and we were getting along better. Really connecting again, I thought, but was it just his guilt or a manipulation tactic? That's what I don't know."

"Could be both."

"Just don't stay because you think you have to do so because you took a vow. Life's too short."

"I know. I need to get back to trial," I tell him in part because it's true, but also because I don't want to talk about this anymore.

I'm the first to arrive back in the courtroom. Coyle and the victim witness coordinator come in next and we chit chat for a few minutes. Though we are "enemies," we can sometimes enjoy each other's company at least in breaks. Regan comes in and gets set up at her station.

"The State calls Dr. Robert Young. Sir, what is your occupation?"

"I'm the chief medical examiner."

"Please tell the jury about your education and experience."

"I attended college at Georgetown and medical school at Johns Hopkins University. I then did a fellowship in pathology and worked as a pathologist in the Commonwealth of Virginia for fifteen years prior to taking this position as the chief medical examiner."

"How long have you been the chief medical examiner?"

"For five years."

"Did you conduct the autopsy of Rachel Graves?"

"Yes, I did."

"What did you learn when you conducted that autopsy?"

"That Ms. Graves was a victim of a homicide and the cause of death was a gunshot wound to the abdomen. She didn't die from the original wound but from an infection she received after the surgery at the hospital, but for the gunshot wound, she would not have died."

Coyle finishes and I start right in. "Dr. Young, did you perform toxicology analysis on Ms. Graves?"

"Objection, relevance."

The judge looks at me and I answer before he actually asks." "Your Honor, the state of mind of the victim is relevant. Particularly relevant and material to my client's state of mind since we are pursuing an affirmative defense of self-defense."

"Objection overruled. You may answer."

"Yes, I did a toxicology exam and she had Xanax, methamphetamine, and marijuana in her system."

Those long cross-examinations you see on television aren't realistic or fruitful, especially with professional witnesses. You could do more harm than good.

"State calls Aaron West." The victim witness coordinator escorted Mr. West in. He's wearing jeans and a t-shirt: I'm sure not what the prosecution was hoping he would wear.

"Mr. West, can you tell us what your relationship with Ms. Graves is?"

"She was my old lady. We'd been together about five years." I hate the term 'old lady' I think to myself.

"Where were you two on the night of May 17?"

"We were at our home on highway 3."

"Who all was there?"

"Me and Rachel and then James brought the defendant with him."

"What were you all doing?" Coyle asks.

"We were just all sitting around talking."

"Did something unusual happen that night?"

"After James left, the Defendant started babbling about people being out to get him and then said that we were in on it. Then, he turned and shot me and shot Rachel."

"When did you first see his gun?"

"Right before he shot me."

"Did you have a gun?" T

"Yes, I had my .45."

"What kind of gun did the Defendant have?" He's trying to make the testimony of this witness clearer and more memorable for the jury as well as not open too many doors for cross.

"He had a .9mm pistol,"."

"Where was your gun when the Defendant pulled out his?"

"It was in my holster at my waist where it always is."

"What prompted the Defendant to shoot you?"

"Nothing at all, he just started talking nonsense and shot me and killed Rachel."

"What happened after he shot you?"

"I fell down and then heard the next gunshot and Rachel scream. I tried to get to her, and the Defendant went into another room and came back in the room. I screamed at him to leave and fired a warning shot at him, and he took off running out the door and I followed him just to make sure he was leaving and went back to Rachel and called 911,."

Coyle's tone softens, "Can you describe Rachel's injuries?"

"She was shot in the stomach. She was bleeding heavily, and I couldn't get it to stop. She had surgery and later got an infection and died."

"What about you?"

"I was shot in the shoulder. It still hurts to this day."

"You're a drug dealer, aren't you?" I start off strong.

"No, I'm not,.."

"You pled guilty to distribution of illegal controlled dangerous substances, correct?"

"Yes because I made a deal with the prosecutor."

"Are you saying you lied to the court when you pled guilty?" I

"No, I had the drugs in my house."

"Your Honor, may I approach?"

"Yes, Counsel, you have free reign."

I move toward the witness with the pictures of the crime scene and pictures of text messages from his phone. "Mr. West, I'm handing you Defense Exhibits 1-5. Have you seen these pictures before?"

"Yes."

"Can you tell the jury what these pictures are one by one, starting with 1?" I ask.

"Exhibit 1 is a picture of the living room of my house. 2 is a picture of the office in my house. 3 is a picture of the front yard of my house. 4 is a picture of the driveway. 5 is a picture of text messages from my phone," he says.

"Do those pictures accurately represent all of those things?" I ask for purpose of getting them admitted.

I follow the rest of the procedure to get these admitted. "Mr. West, please read exhibit 5," I tell him.

"First message, 'how many oxys do you have?' Second message, 'as many as you need. $20 a pill. Third message, 'Be there in 30. Fourth message, 'I want to buy an 8 ball.' Fifth message, '$250 have to be here in the next hour," he reads. I put this in mostly so I can use this later in closing arguments.

"Can you explain to the jury why there is blood on the porch?"

"Because I chased the defendant out. I was afraid he would finish us off."

"So, it's your testimony that the Defendant continued shooting at you after he shot Rachel?" I ask suspecting he will lie.

"Yes, he did. He was a mad man, I shot until he was down, or we would be dead."

"You shot him in the back of the thigh Mr. West, how was he a danger to you?"

"He kept stopping and shooting back."

"So, the police would have found evidence of that outside then?"

"They should have."

"Would you be surprised to know that they didn't?"

"Yes, they must have because that's what happened."

"Were you high that night?"

"No, I was not."

"You do know that the hospital took your blood and tested for drugs, right?"

"No, I didn't until you said something at that last hearing.

"Mr. West, are these your medical records from the trauma hospital?"

"I haven't seen these before."

"But they appear to be medical records about you from that night would you agree?"

"That's what it says, but I wouldn't know."

"What would you say if I told you these medical records show you tested positive for methamphetamine and Xanax?"

"I don't know. I wasn't on anything. It must be a mistake."

"So, the police, the hospital, and Mr. Flowers all made mistakes is that your testimony?"

"I guess so."

"Nothing further." *Yes that cross went well.*

Coyle didn't redirect and judge adjourned us for the day. "Members of the jury, I would remind you to stay off social media; do not watch the news; do not read the newspapers; and do not discuss this case with anyone."

CHAPTER 23

We return to the record this morning and Coyle calls Investigator Jason Goins to the stand. The Investigator comes in dressed in a suit. Detectives typically are in plain clothes rather than a uniform, so this is not a surprise. I like this detective. Usually, most detectives I get along with. They usually have more experience and follow the rules rather than the patrol or rookie cops. I ignore all the introductory questions about his background because I already know all of this from the preliminary hearing. Now, he starts getting to the investigation part.

"Investigator Goins, what did you see when you arrived on the scene of the shooting?"

"By the time I arrived all of the shooting victims had already left the scene. There several patrol officer and crime scene technicians there. I had talked to the officers, but I had to prepare a search warrant and get a judge's approval to search the residence. As I walked the scene, I saw lots of shells and casings, a gun, and blood outside. Inside I saw drugs, pipes, more guns, and more blood inside the house."

"You took pictures and prepared the diagram of the scene?"

"Yes, I did."

"In the course of your investigation, what did you determine happened?"

"I determined that the Defendant fired two shots from

LADY LAWYER

his .9mm. One was removed by the doctors from Rachel Graves's abdomen. I assume the other is still inside Mr. West. In addition, I discovered that Mr. West unloaded his .45."

"Who did you determine was the aggressor in this situation?"

"The Defendant,."

"Why?"

"Based in part on statements of the victims, as well as the fact that the Defendant came to their home armed. He also didn't call 911. He attempted to flee."

"The Defendant made a statement to you about happened, didn't he?"

"Yes, he did while at the hospital."

"What did he tell you?"

"The Defendant said that Mr. West became paranoid and threatened him with his gun. The Defendant then said he shot Mr. West. Next, he shot Ms. Graves because he believed she was going to shoot."

"Did you believe him?"

"Objection, relevance. The witness's determination about credibility doesn't matter. That's for the jury to decide."

"State?" Judge Benson asks for a response.

"This witness is a trained investigator who can give testimony based on his training and experience whether or not he believed the witness was telling the truth."

"Sustained."

I walk toward the witness and show him the diagram. I also uncover and enlarge it on the screen for the jury to see. "Mr. Goins, this exhibit has already been admitted, you were the one that prepared it right?"

"Yes, I did."

"Now it was my client that had the .9mm gun correct?"

"Yes."

"Mr. West had a .45 correct?"

"Yes."

"Are there any .9mm shell casings on this diagram?"

"There are none."

"Can you now show where all there were .45 caliber bullets?"

"So, Investigator when you interviewed Mr. West, did he tell you that my client was shooting back at him when he chased him out?"

"Yes."

"Can you explain why there are .45 casings firing in the direction the Defendant ran but none back in the direction of Mr. West?"

"No, I can't."

"As an investigator does the physical evidence support Mr. West's account that the Defendant was firing back at him?"

"No, it does not."

"Didn't Mr. West also originally tell you that the drugs belonged to the Defendant?"

"Yes, he did."

"Did your investigation reveal who the drugs belonged to?"

"The larger quantities of drugs were put back in a safe

and we did not find any fingerprints or DNA belonging to the Defendant. There were smaller quantities and residue in pipes and bags left out. I determined that all parties were likely using the drugs prior to the shooting, but that the drugs found in the safe belonged to Mr. West."

"Do you have any physical evidence that contradicts what the Defendant told you?"

"No, but based on my investigation I thought it unlikely given that he had a minor gunshot wound when running away and that the victims were shot in the home."

"But there is no physical evidence to contradict the Defendant's version?"

"No,."

I have more things or points I want to make, but I like to summarize it all in closing. Some people do long crosses and belabor every point. I find it better to make the points and bring it together in closing arguments. When I finish, Coyle doesn't ask further questions and rests his case.

"Members of the jury we will take our morning break. Return to the jury room in thirty minutes."

After the jury left. "Ms. Jones, any record?"

"Yes, Your Honor, I would demur to the evidence and move for a directed verdict," I state. I have no reason to believe this will be granted but must raise it all the same.

"Overruled. Ms. Jones, does your client intend to testify?"

"Yes, Your Honor."

"Let's have our Boykin hearing now then. Call your witness."

"Sir for the record your name is Matthew Flowers, correct?"

"Yes."

"You and I have discussed your right to remain silent and not to testify in this case, haven't we?"

"Yes, we have."

"You understand that it is your right to choose whether to testify or not?"

"Yes, this is my choice."

"You also understand that the prosecutor will be able to cross-examine you?"

"Yes, I do."

"Has anyone forced you or coerced you into testifying?"

"No."

"Anyone bribed you with anything to testify?"

"No."

"Are you under the influence of any drugs or alcohol today?"

"No, I am not."

"Are you on any medication that affects your ability to understand your rights?"

"No."

"Do you have any mental health problems or been treated by any mental health professionals?"

"No, I don't."

Judge Benson looks at Mr. Flowers and inquires, "You do understand that no one can make you testify, correct?"

"Yes sir, I do."

"Ok, you may step down." See you all back after the break and start with the defense."

"We are back on the record after our morning break and the State has rested. Defense call your first witness."

"The Defense calls Matthew Flowers."

"Sir please state your name for the record," I start with the usual.

"Matthew Flowers."

"How old are you?"

"Nineteen."

"Mr. Flowers, would you take us through what you were doing on May 17th of last year?"

"That day I worked on my grandpa's farm and then I met up with my friend James. He then suggested we go to his friend Aaron's."

"Why were you going to his friend Aaron's?"

"We were going to get some drugs."

"Matt, how long have you been doing drugs?"

"I tried marijuana first at sixteen. Some friends introduced me to methamphetamine when I was seventeen. I haven't done any since I went to jail."

"When you got there to Mr. West's home that night, did you do any drugs?"

"Yes, all of us smoked a bowl of methamphetamine when we first arrived."

"Who do you mean by all of us?"

"Aaron, Rachel, James and me."

"What happened after that?"

"We were sitting around talking and smoking. James bought an eight ball from Aaron and left but said he would be back."

"Why did he leave you there?"

"I really don't know. He was going to sell the eight ball and come back. I'm not sure. I wasn't aware of what all James and Aaron had going on between them. I didn't ask."

"After James left, what happened?"

"Rachel asked me if I wanted to do a bump. I told her that I had never done that before."

I stop him before he continues. "What do you mean by a bump?

"A bump is a shot of meth."

"Did you do a bump?"

"Yes, Rachel loaded the syringes for me, her, and Aaron. I've never shot up before, so it was a lot stronger than what I'm used to doing."

"What happened after that?"

"Aaron started acting strangely. There were some surveillance monitors inside his living room. He then said there were people coming to get us and that we needed to go outside and check the grounds. Aaron and I did that but didn't find anyone. He then started spouting off that I was going to rob him, and that James brought me to set him up. He started pacing back and forth. I told him that wasn't true, but then he turned around and pointed the gun at me. I had my gun in my hand from when we went outside. When I saw him point the gun, I fired at him. Then, out of the corner of my eye I see Rachel moving and getting her gun. I yelled, 'Don't do it.' She continued to pull the gun up in my direction, so I shot her."

"What were you feeling when you fired those shots?"

"Scared. I was afraid I might be shot or killed. I did what I had to do."

"No further questions, your Honor." *That went about as well as it could have.*

"Mr. Flowers, only three people know what happened that night and one of them is dead is that correct?"

"Objection, argumentative."

"Sustained."

"So, it's your testimony that your friend James just left you there at this place you had never been before and with people you didn't know?"

"That's what happened."

"Isn't it true that your plan was to rob them of their drugs?"

"No and I didn't take anything from them."

"You shot two people in cold blood, didn't you?"

"No, I only shot because they were both about to shoot me?"

"You were the one claiming you heard a gunshot, weren't you?"

"No, that was Aaron."

"Isn't is true that you were high that night and you didn't know what was going on?"

"We were all high, but it was Aaron's paranoia that led to the shooting. I wish I had never done any drugs. I wish this hadn't happened. I have to live with the fact that I killed someone. If I could take it back I would, but I had no other choice."

"Why didn't you call 911, Mr. Flowers, if your shooting was justified?"

"Before I had a chance, Aaron shot at me and missed and then chased me out of the house and kept shooting until I was hit in the back of my leg and went down."

"Why didn't you call 911 after you went down?"

"Because I couldn't find my phone. I was bleeding and in pain. I think I passed out at some point."

"You have an answer for everything, don't you?"

"Objection, Your Honor."

"I'll withdraw."

"Mr. Flowers, you went to a stranger's home armed with a gun planning to purchase and use drugs correct?"

"Yes, I always carry a gun."

"You didn't think that was dangerous idea to bring a gun to your drug dealer's house?"

"I didn't really think about it."

"You didn't think bringing a gun into someone else's house might incite violence. You went there with felonious intent, didn't you?"

"I don't know what that means." he answers without sounding like a smart alec.

"You knew you were going to commit a crime by your own admission, and you took a gun, what did you expect to happen?"

"I didn't expect anything to happen. It was just another day."

"I'm done with this witness."

"Any redirect, counsel."

"No, your Honor, and the Defense rests."

"Members of the jury, we are going to break for lunch as we have some things to complete. Return at 2:00 P.M. to the jury room. Remember, do not discuss this case with anyone or with each other until I submit to you. Thank you."

As soon as the jury exited, Judge Benson states, "I have received proposed self-defense instructions from the Defendant. I have prepared jury instructions of my own. State, do you have any additional ones that you request outside of the normal ones?"

"Nothing outside the normal ones."

"I will have drafts available in fifteen minutes." With that, he leaves the bench.

CHAPTER 24

REGAN

Oh no! I see my husband's number on the text messages exhibit asking to buy the drugs. I can't believe this. This must be why he has been acting out of control. I knew something had to be going on. I'm still in my shock when I hear, "Regan, you want to grab lunch?"

"I've got to run home and take care of a couple things, rain check?"

"I'll see you back here this afternoon awaiting a verdict anyway." Lindsey smiled at me.

I rush home. I'm not sure where to start looking and not sure what I will do if I find anything. I start in his workout room. I don't see any hiding places necessarily, but I start feeling along the weight benches. I don't find anything there, so I move on to his toolboxes in the garage. I open all of them and find nothing out of the ordinary. I go back to our master bathroom and start looking in his shaving kit. Still nothing. Could he be hiding it in his clothes? But I do all our laundry, so that doesn't make sense.

I start going through the pockets of his jackets and find nothing but candy wrappers, scraps of paper, and miscellaneous stuff. I don't find anything of value. Then it hits me the most logical place for him to hide something from me would be in his truck. I don't drive it often at all and when we go somewhere together, I'm not searching through anything.

How am I going to prove this? I sit and think and come to it, I will just start detailing his truck tonight. That will give me an excuse to search.

I try to calm down. I make a peanut butter sandwich and eat about half of it before heading back to the courthouse. I have to focus because I've got to transcribe the closing arguments, but I think of another place to look: the guest room. His video games and some of his other toys are in that room. I start to look through the entertainment center in the guest room. As I'm opening the drawers and opening the games, not finding anything, I'm about to give up when see something silver sticking up. I throw the rest of the games out and pull up a secret compartment hidden in the bottom of this draw to find a pipe that appears to be like the ones used for meth from the pictures I have seen. I also find several pills. I'm so engrossed in what I'm seeing I don't even know anyone is there until I am wrenched up off the ground by the neck.

"What the hell do you think you're doing? Going through my things? Did you find what you're looking for? You wanting to turn me in?" He screams all of these questions while holding me up by the neck with my legs dangling. My air supply is cut off. He puts me down and gulp air. "Are you going to answer me?"

"I saw your number on this drug dealer's phone messages in this trial I'm transcribing today . . ." I try to explain but before I can even finish, he slaps me so quick I don't even see it coming as I fall to the floor.

"You're lying. Why were you in here?"

"Trying to see if you had any drugs here. I found this pipe and these pills. What are you doing, Chris?" I

"Don't question me. This is none of your business. Get and stay the hell out of this room." His voice is like a howl and he pushes me down again. I try to walk out of the room and cut around him.

He follows me. "You know that is my room and my stuff. How many times have I told you not to touch my stuff?"

"If you didn't have anything to hide it wouldn't matter. Doing meth and pills? I can't even believe you!"

"You need an attitude adjustment!" He throws me on the bed and I'm not sure what is about to happen, but I realize he is pulling off his belt. "Maybe this will remind you not to talk to me that way." He hits me with the belt across my butt once, twice, three times, four times, five times. I let out a yelp after the first one and just stay still in stunned silence.

He is dead silent then. I think even realizing he went too far. It really hurt. I stand back up and realize that I'm crying. "I have to get back to work. They are doing closing arguments."

"You can't go looking like that."

"I'll put more make-up on and fix my hair. No one will know." I move toward the master bathroom. *That really hurt. I can't be limping around. I take 4-200 mg ibuprofen.* I fix my make-up and hair and put on fresh lipstick and I realize it's 2:00. *Damn it! I should already be there.* I hurry toward the front door and I hear Chris call out, "I'll see you tonight."

What am I going to do? He's out of control. He's using drugs. He clearly isn't in any state of mind to talk about it. If I leave him, that's going to be a huge scene too. I doubt he's just going to go along with it. I don't want to get him in trouble, but should I tell the police. What if I do that and he's gotten rid of everything and they don't do anything? Then he'll just be angrier. There's no way he'll move out of the house on his own. His name is on all the bills. I don't know that I make enough money to make it on my own. I do love him. I love the person he really is. The violence has gotten progressively worse though. I don't know what to do. I'm not one of those women. I'm not a victim. I'm not helpless. I don't want the people that I work with every day at the courthouse to know about this. If I file for a protective order or a divorce, it will come out. Then they will pity me. I can't stand pity. If he gets help and changes then no one would understand if I went back and they would judge me for that too. Even Lindsey. She's been supportive, but what if she abandons me too? Then, I'll be left with no one.

Lindsey is calling and I realize I've missed several other calls. *Pull it together girl. No one has to know. At least not now.*

CHAPTER 25

  I decide to just run home during the break to practice my closing argument and just grab a snack. I don't get too nervous in trials, but closings really tie it all together. Believing you have an innocent client adds pressure to an already stressful situation. I believe I've tried the best case I can, though looking back, I always miss something, because I'm only human. Matt trusts me with his life. If the jury convicts him of murder, he will receive life in prison. I try to stop thinking about that and just focus on my closing and making sure I know all the points I must hit. I write out my closings word for word, but I also do bullet points, because I never want to read to the jury. I want to talk to them, but I don't want to leave anything out either.

  When I get back to the courtroom, Matt is already at the table. "How are you feeling, Matt?" I

  "You've got this right, Lins?"

  "I think we've put on a good defense, and I'll give it all I can in this closing. I think you're in a good position, but you can never what a jury is going to do but have faith." I can't promise him anything, but I also don't want him to give up either.

  "Just keep fighting for me."

  "I will." The prosecution crew comes in at that point, so I focus on getting in the zone. We sit there waiting until 2:10 and no one has come out yet. Sherrie signals for Coyle and me to come into chambers. "Regan isn't here yet and I've called her office and cell with no answer. Do you know anything?"

  "No, she told me she was going home for lunch and had to take care of a couple things. Let me try her." Shivers go through me because it is not like her to be late, particularly for a trial. The phone is ringing and ringing and almost goes to voicemail when she picks up. "Lindsey, I'm walking in the building. I'm so sorry."

"We were beginning to get worried."

"I'm ok. I'll be right there."

I see her then and she doesn't look right. "Regan, are you ok?"

"Yes, just frazzled because I'm running so late. Go break a leg."

"Ok, we'll talk later." I tell her while Coyle and I both go back into the courtroom.

The Judge, bailiff, and Regan come in shortly after, and Judge Benson seats us and sends his bailiff to get the jury. He reads the jury instructions or the law that the jury must use to decide its verdict. I stop following along after a while because I'm ready to speak, but the State gets to go first and last. I have to be prepared to combat what I can in my closing. As Judge Benson finishes reading his closings instructions, he again tells the jury that what the lawyers say is not evidence and tells the State to proceed.

Coyle heads to the podium with his notes. "Ladies and Gentlemen, there are no swans in the sewers. The Defense has certainly attacked the credibility of Mr. West as a drug dealer and Ms. Graves for using drugs, but the Defendant was not innocent either. If the Defendant hadn't gone there to buy and use drugs himself, none of this would have happened. What about his credibility? It is undisputed that the Defendant shot two people. He murdered Rachel Graves. He shot Aaron West. The Defendant got high and shot two people. The fact that he was using drugs is not an excuse for murdering one person and shooting another. We heard the Defendant testify that he was acting in self-defense, but this is the first time we have ever heard this story. It's a pretty convenient story that unfortunately one of the witnesses didn't survive long enough to combat it.

The judge read the law to you but let me highlight what the State had to prove to you for you to find the Defendant guilty. To find him guilty of murder 2, the State had to prove the following things: 1) death of a human; 2) caused by conduct that was imminently dangerous to another; 3) the conduct was that of the defendant's; 4) the conduct evinced a depraved mind in extreme disregard of human life; 5) conduct is not done with the intention of taking the life of a particular individual. It is undisputed that Rachel Graves passed away. The imminently dangerous conduct was taking a gun with him to purchase and use drugs and then pulling that gun out with other people consuming drugs and that were also armed. The Defendant admits taking the gun to this home where he knew they were going to purchase drugs. The Defendant shot Rachel Graves causing her death though it may not have been intent to kill her, but he pointed a gun and shot her. Pointing a gun at anyone is inherently dangerous. He disregarded any risks associated with using methamphetamine and carrying a gun. That is a depraved mind. That is second degree murder.

As to count 2, assault and battery with a deadly weapon, we must show three things: 1) an assault and battery, 2) upon another person, 3) with a deadly weapon. The assault and battery occurred when the bullet from the Defendant's gun struck Aaron West, who is the other person. The deadly weapon in this case is the .9 mm gun that the Defendant had in his possession when paramedics and police arrived on the scene. Ladies and gentlemen, this Defendant is guilty beyond a reasonable doubt on both counts and I ask you to return that verdict. Thank you." Coyle finishes his first close and sits down.

Judge Benson tells me to proceed. I walk to the podium with my notes, but I step to the side of it so I can look directly at the jurors. "Three people on methamphetamine. Three people with guns. Three people were shot. Mr. Flowers is a drug addict and we admit that. He along with Mr. West and Ms. Graves were using drugs that night. They all made choices last night. One unfortunate side effect of using methamphetamine can be paranoia and hallucinations. Mr. West became paranoid and convinced that Mr. Flowers was going to rob him. He pointed a gun at him. Mr. Flowers had to decide right then and there whether to shoot or wait to be shot. He shot to save his life.

He shot again to stop Ms. Graves from shooting him. This is the classic self-defense situation.

Now, ladies and gentlemen, you don't have to like my client. My client along with the deceased and Mr. West were all using methamphetamines that night. Mr. West lied to you and this Court when he said Mr. Flowers was shooting back at him when Mr. Flowers was trying to leave. Mr. West also lied to the police when he tried to claim that all the drugs and paraphernalia were my client's. The physical evidence flatly contradicts Mr. West's account. The physical evidence supports what Mr. Flowers told you. He acted in self-defense. He chose to live. He acted like any reasonable person would have done in his same situation.

The State tried to imply the Defendant was hiding something because he didn't tell this story until today, but that is absolutely his constitutional right in the United States of America. He didn't have to speak to police. He didn't have to testify here today and the fact that he didn't give his account to anyone other than his lawyers cannot be used against him. He was being smart and exercising his rights.

We raised the defense of self-defense, and it is the duty of the State to disprove that my client acted in self-defense beyond a reasonable doubt. They have completely failed to meet that burden. This case reeks of reasonable doubt: lying witnesses; everyone involved using methamphetamine. I have little doubt the State will tell you to use your common sense and I ask you to do that same thing. Your common sense tells you that you can't believe anything that Aaron West said. The State's whole case rests on him, and he is just not believable. The State had to prove that my client did not act in self-defense beyond a reasonable doubt. They didn't even come close. You took an oath to uphold the law and to return a verdict of not guilty if the State didn't prove their case. They have fallen miserably short of their burden. Return a verdict of not guilty and let Mr. Flowers move on with his life. Thank you." I look each of them in the eye and sit down.

Coyle begins his rebuttal with the notes he was scribbling during my closing and heads to the podium. "Let's start with that common sense that Ms. Jones told you to use. Common sense says if the Defendant thought he had acted in self-defense; he would have stopped to call 911 rather than running off. The Defendant was using methamphetamine. His testimony up there was completely self-serving to avoid a life sentence in prison. His credibility and motive to lie is extremely high. There are no perfect witnesses in this trial, but it was the Defendant who, by his own admission, came armed to buy drugs. It was the Defendant who did a shot of methamphetamine for the first time that night. It was the Defendant who shot two people-killing one of them. This was not self-defense. It was an execution of Ms. Graves. You may ask why but like we talked about in the beginning, the State doesn't have to prove the motive or why the Defendant shot these people. Just have to prove that he did and without justification. The victim Ms. Graves didn't survive her encounter with the Defendant to be able to give her testimony today. This wasn't self-defense. He didn't attempt to render aid to either individual. He didn't seek to disarm them. Nothing about how he acted after the shooting indicates self-defense. He just ran away. Innocent men don't run away. Return a verdict of guilty that your common sense tells you the evidence supports. Send a message to the Defendant that you don't get to shoot two people and get away with it. Find him guilty. Thank you," he says and sits down.

"Ladies and gentlemen, the trial is concluded, and you will retire to the jury room to start your deliberations. Start by selecting a foreperson. My bailiff will take you up. You will also have to leave all cell phones and electronic devices with her," the judge says, and we all stand for them to exit the room. The jurors left the room at 2:28. We will see how long they deliberate.

I look at Matt and say, "Now we wait," I say and stretch.

"How long do you think?" Matt asks.

"I don't know. It's different each time. Only thing time tells us is they made up their mind quickly or they struggled. It doesn't tell us which way it is going. I'm going to go get a snack," I tell him and give him a pat on the back.

The district attorney's office crew heads back to their office. The spectators are starting to leave. The spectators are other attorneys and courthouse staff that like to watch the closing arguments. Nick is there and is waiting on me, "Well what did you think?"

"Your story is better. You've got lots of doubt. Jury just may not believe anyone and find him not guilty. I don't see how they find him guilty, but it is hard to let a murder go unpunished."

"Yeah I hope so. He's been in jail for nine months. I hope if they acquit him that he will stay sober and turn over a new leaf."

"Unless he wants to stay sober and get some treatment, just because he's been sober in jail, you know, doesn't mean he will stay sober upon release."

"I know. I need to get a snack."

"Ok, I'll be in talking to Sherrie."

"Ok, I'll be back up in a minute." I head downstairs to get a Mountain Dew and a Reese's and then head back to Sherrie's office. Judge is back in his office now too.

Sherrie asks me how late of a night do I think that I will have. I joke that they will come back with a quick not guilty.

We hear a bell ring once, which means the jury has a question. We call Coyle and tell him to come back. Turns out he was across the hall in a different judge's office. Sherrie heads upstairs to the jury room and Judge Benson, Coyle, and I wait in judge's chambers to see what the question is. A few minutes later, Sherrie comes down and reads the questions, "Does self-defense have to be proven beyond a reasonable doubt?"

"I don't think you can answer that."

"Judge, I think just answer you have all of the instructions that you need."

Judge Benson types up that answer for Sherrie to take up.

"I guess we know what they are talking about."

"Yeah but which way. I think probably your way."

"I don't know, Robert. Your closing was good as well. It is a murder case."

He goes back to his office. I sit back down in Sherrie's office. Nick says, "Sounds like a good sign for you."

"Hopefully so. I need to go tell Matt." I walk back into the courtroom and try to encourage him..

Waiting on a verdict is so nerve-wracking: absolutely nothing I can do now, but perfectionist that I am, I replay the trial in my head. I think and overthink of any objections I missed, questions I forgot to ask, or if I stumbled over any words in closings. I pace around the room. I get bored of that and walk up to Regan's office and knock. I text her, "Hey girl, where are you? I'm worried about you."

"I'm driving around. Thinking. I'll talk to you more later." I go back to the courtroom to play candy crush. The jury has been out about an hour and a half at this point. Will comes in. "Still waiting, Lins? I heard your closing was good."

"Thanks. I think we have a good chance."

"I hope you win."

"For me as well as you."

"A loss would negatively affect his campaign."

By this time, more staff members come back over with Coyle to wait on the verdict. With that Will leaves and asks me to keep him posted. It's awkward enough for me to wait around with this tense campaign, but for Will it would be worse.

Finally, we hear two rings which signals a verdict. The time has arrived.

Regan comes back so we can go back on the record. Judge Benson comes out and says, "During the break, the jury sent one question in..."

I'm not really paying attention at this point because my heart is pounding. These last few moments are the worse. The jury comes down then and some look and some don't. That cliche about if they don't look, it's guilty, doesn't holdup.

Judge Benson then addresses the jury. "Have you selected a foreperson?"

A man in his fifties stands up and advises he was the

foreman and that the verdict was unanimous. "Hand the verdict form to the bailiff. Judge Benson orders and Sherrie takes the verdict form to him. Judge looks at it and commands. "Defendant, you will rise while the Clerk reads the verdict."

The Clerk begins, "In the Matter of the State v. Matthew Flowers on the first count of murder in the second degree, we the jury, empaneled and sworn, find as follows: the Defendant is not guilty. In the Matter of the State v. Matthew Flowers on the second count of assault and battery with a deadly weapon, we the jury, empaneled and sworn, find as follows: the Defendant is not guilty."

"Ladies and gentlemen of the jury, thank you for your service. Our system would not work without our citizens performing this duty. You are free to go. The lawyers always like to speak to the jury, but you are certainly not obligated. If anyone is critical of your service, let me know. With that, the Defendant is also free to go."

Matt grabs me in a bear hug and lifts me up with excitement,. "Thank you, thank you so much! I can't believe it! I feel like the white O.J."

"I'm so happy for you!"

His mom Glenda runs up at this point and hugs Matt and me. *This is a great feeling of giving him his life back.*

I separate at that point and approach Coyle. "Robert, you tried a good case."

"You did too. Congratulations."

CHAPTER 26

Regan comes up to me then. "Lins, I need to talk to you. Can we go somewhere?"

"Sure. I could really use a drink. I also need to update people on the verdict. Can you drive?"

"Yeah, that's fine. I'd rather not be alone anyway,"."

"Regan, what's wrong?"

"Let's get to the restaurant and we'll talk."

"Let me drop this file off at my office. I'll meet you at your car," I tell her and walk quickly over to my office. While on the way, I call my mom and tell her the good news.

I get into Regan's car then and while we drive to the restaurant, I text Nick and Will and let them know the verdict and then the crime-writer from the local newspaper called me.

"Hello?"

"Yes, this is Shirley Shore from the paper, and I am writing a story about the case. Do you have time to answer a few questions?"

"Yes, I do."

"Do you think the jury got it right?"

"Yes, I absolutely do. My client, though not perfect, acted in self-defense. He advises he never intends to touch drugs again. I think this case was overcharged to begin with and the District Attorney's Office took months before even filing the case. I think the jury also saw that the State's chief witness was a liar. This restores my faith in the justice system. This a perfect example of the system upholding the presumption of innocence despite the odds."

"How do you think this case affects the ongoing political campaign for district attorney?"

" think it gives the public another reason to vote for change. Trials, such as this one, are very costly. In the last two years since Mr. Coyle became First Assistant, Defendants have taken many more cases to trial due to the inability to work cases out. In addition, Mr. Coyle doesn't seem to share the view of the public in regard to criminal justice reform." I am more than happy to put in a plug that helps Will in his bid for district attorney.

As we walk in, I notice Regan is limping. "What's wrong with you? Why are you limping?"

"It's nothing."

"It's definitely something."

"I'll tell you when we get seated."

Once we are seated, I ask "What is going on?"

"During the trial, I looked at the text messages you introduced and the number that was asking for the drugs was Chris's."

I'm speechless not knowing what to say.

"I turned down lunch today to go home and see if I could find any evidence of it and right after I find a pipe and several pills, he comes home and finds me. He completely lost it."

"What did he do?"

"It's not important, but the worst it has ever been. I'm afraid to go home,"."

"You will not go home. You will come home with me."

"Your house will be the first place he will look."

"But you won't be alone. Justin and I will be there, and we won't let him in. Do you want to make a police report?"

"No, I don't want to involve the police. I don't want other people knowing about this."

"What about a protective order?"

"I don't know. I really don't want to do anything right now, but I just don't want to go home right now."

"You will come home with me for the time being until you decide what you want to do. I can't believe that and that you learned it in my trial!"

"I know! Congratulations! You tried a great case. How does it feel?"

"It's such a good feeling. Not only to win, but to save someone's life"

My strawberry daiquiri, along with our chips and salsa, and Regan's phone starts vibrating. "Is that him?"

Regan looks at her phone. "Yes, he's calling. I'm sure he is wondering why I'm not home yet. I don't feel like talking to him right now."

I can tell she's anxious, so I change the subject to the election to try to take her mind off of things, but her phone keeps vibrating over and over and I finally offer, "Maybe you should just put it on silent and take the vibrate function off. He's probably going to keep calling."

"I think I'll send him a text and then do that." Before she even gets the vibrate off, I can tell he is answering back.

"How did he take it?" "Not well. He's livid that I'm not home. He's threatening to start destroying everything in the house if I don't come home. He's also saying that he will change the locks so I can't get back in if I don't come home tonight. I'm just going to ignore him for now and let him calm himself down."

"Are you ok?" *What a stupid question.*

"His temper is just out of control. I want to have a normal conversation with him about the drugs and his anger, but I'm walking on eggshells all the time and then he just lost it today. I was truly afraid of what all he might do to me. I'm just really uneasy."

"I'm sure you are. You can stay with Justin and me for as long as you need to."

"Have you told Justin or are we just going to show up? He has a say too."

"I texted him, but he knows better than to complain after what he did."

"How are you two doing?" She asks sincerely even with what she is going through.

"I told him we would try counseling together after this trial was finished. I don't know if we will work out or not. We may just ditch the husbands and become roommates."

"Hey, there could be worse things."

I paid the bill over her objection and we went back to the courthouse to get my car and head home. Justin greeted us at the door. "Regan I changed the bedding in there. Make yourself at home."

"Thanks, Justin," she says, then adds, "Lins, I don't have any extra clothes or anything."

"Bathroom has extras of everything including my make-up which may not be perfect but will work. I'll get some pajama pants and a t-shirt for you,."

She heads back to the extra bedroom. "Thanks for that and while she's here, use the master bathroom with me so she can have her privacy."

"Ok I will. How is she doing?"

"Not well. He was blowing her phone up all through dinner, and I'm sure he still is. He may show up here too."

"I'll deal with him if he does. It will be fine. Congratulations on the trial by the way! I know you worked really hard on it."

"Thank you. I'm thrilled it turned out the right way, but I'm absolutely exhausted and drained. I'm going to get the stuff for her and go ahead and lay down. We'll talk more tomorrow."

"Ok, if you need anything, let me know."

About an hour later, I hear banging on the front door. "Regan, I know you are in there! As I walk into the living room, I see Justin at the front door and answering, "Chris, dude, you need to calm down. Regan doesn't want to see you right now, so just give it some time and go home."

"She's my wife. She's coming with me now!" Chris screams and tries to come through the door, but Justin pushes him back and slams the door quickly.

Justin then says through the door, "Chris, you have thirty seconds to get off my porch, or I will call the police!"

"This isn't over!"

I see a shaking Regan in the living room. "Maybe, I should just go."

"No, Regan, you aren't going anywhere tonight. You are ok."

"I'm going to have to deal with him sometime and it will probably only get worse with more time."

"Or maybe he will calm down."

"I doubt it."

I make us some coffee because none of us are ready to go to sleep yet after that. Justin's body is stiff as he switches channels until he finds a movie to watch. Regan stays awkwardly still for a minute and nervously moves back and forth until she sits down with us. I feel uneasy and on edge. The adrenaline and happy vibes from my victory today have been swept away by my worry and fear for Regan. I'm not just worried about her physically, but mentally and emotionally as well. After the movie was over, we all went to our respective rooms and tried to sleep, but it didn't come easily to any of us.

CHAPTER 27

The next morning when I get up, Regan is sitting in the kitchen drinking a cup of coffee. She looks up at me when I come in. "I need to go home. I need to get some clothes and make-up."

"Are you sure it's safe?"

"He should be at work. If not, I'll call you and we can go in together."

"I'll just go with you now. Give me a couple minutes to get dressed."

We drive over to her house and Chris's truck is not in the driveway, so we go inside and the first thing we notice is that he has indeed destroyed some things. We see two holes in the wall, an upturned living room table, and spills on the wall that looks like liquid that has dried. She gets two large suitcases out. She starts packing clothes, while I start getting her jewelry, make-up, and toiletries. While we are doing that, Regan's phone rings and we both jump because we are on edge.

"It's Chris. I'm going to answer it. I have to talk to him sometime." She then answers it on speaker. "Hello, Chris."

"So, you're leaving me?"

"What?"

"I can see you on the surveillance."

"You have surveillance on the inside of the house? Since when? Why didn't I know about this?"

"Of course, I have surveillance everywhere in case we are ever robbed, so answer the question, are you leaving me?"

"I don't know, Chris, but I need to get away for a while."

"Look, I'm going to overlook you not coming home and staying in another man's house, but you're not leaving me, do you understand?"

"Chris, I wasn't staying with another man. I stayed with Lindsey. You need to get help and get off the drugs. I can't keep living like this."

"Come home and we will talk."

"I need some time, Chris."

"You took a vow, Regan, until death do us part, remember that."

"Goodbye, Chris."

I hug her and demand that we get out of there. We head back to my house to get ready for the day. Will texts me to come in for lunch for a campaign meeting.

I make Regan tag along and Will, Tyler, Regan, Micah, and I sit down for lunch to discuss the final stretch. I brought a calendar of events we need to attend and door knocking lists to divide up. Tyler starts with, "People seem to think we are losing based on Facebook. He has more followers and there's a lot of negativity going around."

"It's just one piece of the overall puzzle. If you look at his posts, it's the same people, which are his core supporters sharing everything. They aren't reaching the voters. Remember, younger people typically don't vote. The older generation, baby boomers and older, may use Facebook, but that is not where they get their information. We are fine. Many people in the community despise our current DA and Coyle by association. Plus, the more they get to know Coyle, the less they will like him. Just like us."

"It's just so hard not to respond and engage with the crazy accusations. I don't feel like the door knocking is doing anything."

"Studies show that it works though. Just trust the tried and true process."

"I think that he's a Republican is really going to be huge. So many people we have encountered said they would never vote for a Democrat for anything. That gives us an advantage."

"It's a big advantage, but we can't get sloppy just because of it either. We have to finish strong. Just a few more weeks guys and our hard work will have paid off."

"I sure hope so. If not, I'm relocating to Colorado."

"On a lighter note, I have to tell you about Will's awkward experience with a child one night at the county fair. He was standing at the table and these kids are walking by and he literally says, in about the creepiest tone imaginable, 'Little girl, would you like some candy?'"

"Look it didn't come out the way I imagined it in my head." We all laughed and exchange some other stories from the campaign.

"I need to go by my office and see how many messages and how much mail has piled up." I announce as I get up to pay the bill.

"I should check in to see when I'm next needed for a trial as well. I think probably tomorrow, but I'll go there while you're at your office."

For the next few minutes, I check through the mail and prioritize what needs to be worked on and put in an appropriate pile. I return a couple calls and grab the files I need, and hear screaming coming from outside. I rush outside and realize Chris is confronting Regan at the car. Before I can even get there, I see him backhand her. At that moment, a couple deputies come running outside of the courthouse having seen the whole thing.

"Sir, put your hands behind your back." A deputy orders Chris.

Startled, Chris moves back away from Regan. "Look this isn't any of your concern."

"Sir, you made it our problem by attacking one of our courthouse employees outside the courthouse."

Another deputy guides Regan in my direction. "Are you ok? Do you need medical treatment?"

"No, I'm fine."

"Who is that?"

"My husband Chris."

Deputy Austin is over talking to Chris at that time and signals Deputy Lewis over to him. They talk for a couple minutes and then we see Deputy Austin walk Chris over to the courthouse.

Deputy Lewis comes back and says, "Deputy Austin has arrested him and will be transporting him to the jail on charges of domestic assault and battery. He will at least spend the night, but bond will be set in the morning and could be posted at any time, so if you don't feel safe, use this time to get your things and make other arrangements. We can put you in touch with a domestic violence advocate to help you if you want."

Regan's face is blank like she isn't even hearing a word he is saying. I can tell she is overwhelmed, so I speak up for her, "Deputy, I'll talk with her more about that. We have gotten some of her things and she stayed with me last night. I'll take care of her."

"Regan if you can come fill out a statement when you are feeling better tomorrow, but even if you don't want to press charges. We witnessed this assault and it should be on video so the District Attorney's Office will be able to go forward with the charges without you. Take care of yourself."

Regan is still frozen to the spot having only nodded one time. "Regan, honey, let's go home. It's gonna be ok."

I'm not sure what to do to help her. She looks in shock. I know she's in pain. I don't if I should try to snap her out of it and talk to her or let her be for the moment. I mean I've dealt with clients that have been victims but not immediately afterwards and this isn't a client. This is Regan, my best friend. I don't want to alienate her, so I drive us back to my house in silence. As we walk into the house, she says, "I think I'd like to go home and be alone for a while."

"Are you sure? You can't be ok."

"No, I'm not ok, but I just want to be in my own space and think for a while." She begs and walks back to the spare room where she slept last night. I feel so helpless. She returns to the living room a few minutes later with her bags.

"I understand. I'll check on you in a couple hours though and I'm bringing dinner over tonight."

Just then a realization hits me that I wished Justin were here and that I want our marriage to work. I really believe he made a mistake. We hadn't been working on our marriage. I am partially to blame. I was hyper focused on work and my stuff and not focused on him. I'm not sure I'm ready to tell him that, but I call Dr. James's office to schedule an appointment for the two of us.

CHAPTER 28

About two hours later, my phone rings and it was Judge Clarkson. "Lindsey, how are you doing?"

"I'm doing ok, Judge." I answer, wondering why he is calling.

"I hate to do this to you, but it looks as if all the other trials have gone away except for Mr. Graham's assault and battery with a dangerous weapon. We're going to start Monday morning at 8:30,"."

"No problem, Judge. I know we have trailing dockets. At least this term it's not directly back-to-back this time, I get a weekend in between."

"This is true. Enjoy the little bit of respite and see you Monday."

Well, this one is not with Coyle at least. This is with one of the other assistant district attorneys, Maggie Bailey. She is nice enough. This may be her first jury trial to first chair.

I want to go on over and see Regan, but I just text her, "Hey girl, how are you doing?"

Regan texts back, "I'm okay. Just can't believe he did that in front of the courthouse and that he was arrested! Things will never be the same, but I'm trying to think about moving forward. Do you think we could use this to force him into rehab and anger management?"

"I'm sure that can be done. Something needed to stop him in his tracks and hopefully this is it. How about I get some Italian food and desserts and we pig out in a little bit?"

She texts back a thumbs up. I call Justin and tell him about everything that is going on and that will not be home for dinner. I order us a cheese plate, bottle of wine, spaghetti and meatballs, bread, Caesar salad. Totally unhealthy, but comfort food.

"Regan, I know this hard, but are you going to bond him out?"

"No, I want him to get help, but if gets right back out, he won't."

"Do you think he will be able to get someone else to co-sign for him and get out?"

"Probably his parents. I haven't talked to them. I'll be the enemy. He is their golden boy."

"He won't be allowed to have contact with you so you can stay in the home, but that's likely to cause problems, so you're welcome to stay with us for a while."

"I know, Lins, and I appreciate it, but I have to start dealing with this. I've been living in denial for a long time now." She doesn't look at me when she says this.

"Regan, this is not your fault. You can face the problem with help. You don't have to do it alone. I want you to be safe: both physically and emotionally. But enough of that for now, I brought an old classic favorite, Clueless, to watch."

"It's been forever since I've seen that. Perfect. Thank you for being here. She laughs and squeezes my hand. "Lins, I'm going to call your counselor."

At the end of the movie, I head back home. I call out, "Justin, Justin," as I walk in. Justin comes in the living room. "How is Regan?"

"She's as ok as she can be. Justin, I don't want us to get to that point."

"I would never physically hurt you."

"I know that, but you did hurt me badly, and emotional wounds can be worse. We've been together since we were fifteen and I do love you. I'm still hurt and don't trust you, but I scheduled a marriage counseling appointment for next week. Let's at least try."

"I know I did Lins, and I want the chance to make it up to you and for us to get back to being us."

"We may never get back to how we were when we were

fifteen, because we are different people then, but we can have the best relationship for who we are now."

I feel better than I have in a while about my personal life. I have hope again. I know that Regan is strong and that she will make it through this. I will help her either leave or make sure the district attorney's office makes Chris gets the help he needs and that he never hits her again. I have a renewed determination to help other victims of domestic violence.

Now, I must focus on John Graham's case. He is accused of trying to run over a police officer with a car. The whole case will come down to his intent. He has priors so their offer was twenty years, and he was not having it. I hope to win another acquittal, but if I beat the offer on this one, I will take it as a win. It was a nice one day off, but now I have to concentrate on the next person who needs my help. My work is never done.

Made in the USA
Middletown, DE
21 March 2023